Also by Leone Sperling

Coins for the Ferryman

Mother's Day

Oasis

What about love?

Jamie

This is a collection of primarily personal writing consisting of both published and unpublished pieces. There are newspaper articles dealing with family life, short stories that have been published in Australian anthologies and newspapers and an essay that I was asked to provide for a book about fathers. The subject matter is, therefore, varied. I have written about my parents, my children, single parenting and the somewhat frequent failure of my relationships with men.

Leone Sperling
2014

THE BOOK OF LIFE

Stories and Articles by Leone Sperling

© Leone Sperling 2014

Leone Sperling asserts the moral right to be identified as the author of 'The Book of Life'.

Cover design and typeset by Green Avenue Design.

Published by Cilento Publishing, Australia.

ISBN: 978-0-9925602-2-5

THE CLEAN-UP

(Published in The White Chrysanthemum – Selected by Nancy Keesing –
Angus & Robertson – 1977

Republished in Dear Mum – Angus & Robertson – 1977

Republished in The True Life Story Of … Edited by Craney & Caldwell –
University of Queensland Press - 1981)

I come cautiously to consciousness, burrowing deep in the comfort of my own warmth, covers over my head, savouring the uniqueness of my own smell, celebrating the luxury of sleeping alone.

I wait for the familiar sounds that will shake me to full awareness – a shout, a scream, the footsteps of a child. No sounds. The big house communicates its emptiness.

I am momentarily surprised at my reluctance to face the still, summer day. Suddenly I recall the reason for my solitude on this particular day. The children are sleeping at their father's house because she's coming to help me clean up.

I keep wanting to tell her that it's just in my nature to be sloppy. But I can't tell her that. Even if I did she wouldn't listen to me. It's quite obvious to her that I suffer from some serious defect. Equally obvious that I am in desperate need of her help. The long summer holiday is drawing to a close. She thinks the house ought to be put in order before we all go back to school.

She arrives with my father. Bustling, energetic, bundle of grey efficiency. My father leaves, abandoning me to the good intentions of my mother. He couldn't possibly cope with a clean-up of the magnitude intended for this special day. My god! She's even brought corned beef and tomatoes and lettuce for our lunch. Doesn't she know that I do keep some food in the house?

'Would you like a cup of coffee?' I ask, hoping that I might be able to put off this terrible ordeal or at least delay its beginning.

'No, dear, I think we'd better get started. Let's begin with the children's clothes.'

We go downstairs, tripping our way through the mess that hides the playroom floor, along the hall and into the tall, cool children's room. She notices, but does not comment upon, the fact that I haven't made their beds. Now we start to sort out children's clothes. Large garbage bags fill in no time with the accumulated, worn-out, too-small clothes of the last two years.

'I just have to hang the sheets on the line,' I murmur and escape to the outside, performing this usually detested task as slowly as I can, breathing the still air, lulled by the cicadas' song. I wish I could stay here forever – soft and warm and still.

She calls me back: 'Do you want this or shall I throw it away?' I go back. I look at the things she's discarded in the five minutes I've been away. I recover a pair of perfectly good jeans and a red jumper that will obviously fit some child of mine. It's no good. I have to stay with her while she culls the clothes – otherwise the children will have nothing left to wear. Her driving force is to fill as many green plastic garbage bags as possible.

We press on. Two hours pass. She talks all the time. I don't hear what she's saying. I never have. I say yes every now and again, trying hard to still the scream that keeps rising inside me, seeking to insulate myself against the barrage of words.

'Let's stop for coffee.' I don't wait for her reply but go bounding up the stairs to enjoy a momentary respite while I put the kettle on. I want to show her that I do know how to make a cup of coffee. She follows me, still talking. 'Won't it be nice, dear, to start off the year with an absolutely tidy house. I know it's going to be hard for you. You won't get time. Alone with four children, teaching every day. In my day we had nothing else to do. It was easy to keep a house tidy and clean, but these days it's not so easy ....'

I can't listen. If I listen I'll scream and shout, 'Go away! Go away!' and she'll be hurt and I've no right to hurt her. After all, it's my mess we're cleaning up. She's doing this for me, isn't she?

I listen to her drink her coffee. I listen to her eat her biscuits. She doesn't eat biscuits like anyone else in the world. She doesn't bite them. Her jaws crack them to pieces and she gulps them down unchewed. I don't want to eat a biscuit, but I have to – I take one to defend myself against the sound of her champing. If I don't eat a biscuit I think she'll crack her jaws down on me and eat me up. The hot coffee burns my lips. Her lips are made of asbestos. She's consumed four biscuits and swallowed all her coffee before I've had two sips of mine. 'I'll just clear these dishes away, dear, while you finish your coffee.'

She bounces to the sink, energetic and full of vitality. I want to tell her that I have a washing-up machine but I can't get the words out. She stills me to silence. Even if I did tell her, it wouldn't make any difference. She doesn't believe in machines. She washes last night's dishes thoroughly by hand. I am reluctant to finish my coffee. She goes on talking – something about my aunt. I mustn't listen. If I listen I'm done for.

I look fondly at my lounge-room. The floor is strewn with toys and clothes. What would she say if she saw us sometimes, the children and me? We've only had one month of freedom – one month without the disapproving glare of father. Being newly liberated, we revel in our untidiness. Would she understand if she saw the five of us dancing barefoot in the lounge-room, declaring our freedom to each other? 'This is our house and there's no daddy to tell us to clean up and we can make as much mess as we want to!' and that's exactly what we've done – wallowed gloriously in our own mess. Maybe we have overdone it – it's the end of January and the wrappings from the Christmas presents are still on the floor.

She calls me back. 'Come on, dear, let's get your room done before lunch.' I can't face it. My desk is piled high with books and papers, my clothes lie tumbled on the floor, my shoes flow out of the wardrobe.

'I just have to hang out some more washing!' I fly downstairs and rush outside. I'm going to burst! I take my time. I'm lucky. This load of washing has lots of children's clothes in it – socks and singlets and underpants. It takes a long time. I do it carefully, slowly, bending down to pick up each peg. I drag it out for as long as I can.

I have to go back inside – it's unwise to leave her alone for too long in there. A miracle! What a transformation. The clothes are inside the wardrobe, the shoes arranged in pairs, the papers piled neatly on the desk. I'm worried about the two large garbage bags that bulge in the doorway. What can she have thrown out? I'd better not look. Suddenly I am convinced that if I'm not careful she'll bundle me into one of those big bags – wrap me up and tie the string and throw me out with the rest of the rubbish.

Respite! It's time for lunch. She takes out her corned beef and lettuce and tomatoes. I hadn't noticed before. She's even brought a pineapple, sliced, in a screw-capped jar. I'm allowed to supply the milk for our cups of tea. I decide to fight back. I start to talk. I'm not sure what I'm talking about. I think I tell her that I actually know people who are living on the dole. She's sufficiently shocked to become silent for a moment. I keep talking. It doesn't matter what I'm saying. As long as I don't stop. I go on and on and on. I won't let her say a word. I think I'm defending my life-style.

Now comes the really bad part. We are ready for our assault on the toys. Somehow I survive the clearing of the lounge-room, somehow manage to salvage most of the Christmas toys from the rubbish bags, somehow keep the scream down inside of me, even converse with her – if one can call it conversation to pour the occasional yes or no into the pauses between her endless monologues.

We work for two hours in the playroom. We decimate the toys. Somehow I don't think I'm going to make it. The scream keeps welling up inside me. 'Let's finish the rest tomorrow,' I suggest.

'But dear, we've nearly finished. How can you even think of leaving it for tomorrow.' I want to tell her just how easy it is to leave things for tomorrow. I'm a past master at it. I do it all the time. I can't speak. Even if I could she wouldn't understand. She never leaves anything for tomorrow. I ache from head to foot and she looks as spritely as she did when she arrived. Doesn't she ever get tired? I'm half her age and I'm exhausted.

We work for one more hour. My father arrives. I look at him and he looks at me and I see that he understands.

'Come along, Mummy, it's time we were getting home.'

'We just have to do those boxes in the corner,' she replies. If she touches the boxes in the corner I know I won't be able to keep the scream down. I look at my father and he reads the plea in my eyes.

'She can do those herself tomorrow, Mummy. You've both done quite enough for today.'

She agrees to go. The scream subsides. 'Thank you, thank you, thank you,' I say. I am trying very hard to hold on to myself. I ought to be hospitable. 'Would you like a cup of coffee before you go?'

'That would be nice, dear', says my mother.

'No,' says my father. 'I'll make you a nice cup of coffee when we get home.' I smile him my gratitude. We understand each other.

'Now you have a nice early night, dear,' she says on leaving. 'You've worked very hard today.'

The moment they leave I go into my room and put on a record. I turn the volume up high so that the neighbours won't be able to hear me. And then I let it come – long and loud and hard and strong – I scream and scream and scream – from my guts to my throat it bellows its way free – again and again and again until my head reverberates with its howling and my body shakes with its roar. And then I crawl into my bed and curl myself to sleep soothed by the soft caress of my own warm tears.

The next day the children come back to the miracle of a room full of newly discovered toys. It's like Christmas, only better. Each toy sits in its proper place, all its parts intact. They are duly impressed. All the guns are on the gun shelf. All the cars keep each other company. The baby rejoices over a doll that's been buried for six months. The boys keep murmuring, 'Mummy, look what I've found.' I try to impress upon them that this state of perfection is possible only if we all work at it. Every night every toy has to be put back in its pigeon-hole. The first night they do it lovingly, unasked. The second night I have to ask them to do it. The third night I am met with groans of, 'Gee, Mummy, do we have to?' The fourth night I scream at them. I rant and rave. I sound like a fishwife. They start to look at me as if I'm some kind of monster.

Their attitude is catching. I start to throw my clothes on the floor and to hurl my shoes into the wardrobe. The papers and books begin to pile up on my desk.

Within a week one has to navigate a path from one end of the lounge-room to the other. The toys restore themselves to a state of splendid chaos. I hear plaintive cries of, 'Where's my doll?' and 'I can't find my gun.' I smile contentedly. We laugh together, children and I, and we take off our shoes and kick them in ten different directions across the lounge-room floor and barefoot we dance a hymn to our glorious disorder.

THE BOOK OF LIFE

(Published in Room to Move – Redress Press – Unwin Paperbacks – 1985

Republished in Room to Move – Franklin Watts – New York – 1986

Republished in Eclipsed – Two Centuries of Australian Women's Fiction – Burns & MacNamara – Inprint - Collins Australia – 1988

Recorded and read several times on ABC radio.)

It is Kol Nidre night. Tomorrow is the Jewish Day of Atonement, the day on which God decides whose name will be written in the Book of Life for the following year.

He is 83 years old and he wants to live for another year. Not only does he want to live; he must live. It is his sacred duty to stay alive to look after his wife. His wife is eight years younger than he is and physically fitter but she needs looking after, none the less. They have been married now for 50 years. There was a time when he thought he might not make it to his golden wedding anniversary, but he did make it and now he needs to go on living for at least another year.

His wife has lost hold of her memory. It has flittered out of her grasp. She has entered a twilight timelessness where minutes and hours, days and dates, months and years are meaningless. He must be her constant clock. He is her timekeeper, guardian, father and friend. He unravels her confusion and imposes pattern and order onto her chaos. Without him she could not function in the real world.

He has lost his faith. He has lived his life in goodness, guided by the sure knowledge that God the Father looked down upon him and blessed him. But his wife's deterioration has changed all that. If there is a God, how can He have allowed such a thing to happen? Such a clever woman! Incomprehensible. He has lost his mate, his friend, his 50-year companion. She has retreated, contracted. He cannot crawl for comfort into her inner world.

He has gone through all these married years in peace and harmony. No fights in this marriage; no disagreements; no harsh words. But lately he's been getting impatient, irritated, losing his temper. She must ask him the same questions over and over again in her enormous effort to engrave the answers on her sliding mind. Sometimes he cannot control himself. The irritation builds and mounts and, before he knows it, he explodes in anger. And then she cries and he feels guilty. He keeps reminding himself that she can't help it. It's not her fault. He manages to stay calm most of the time. The thing that upsets him most is the enormous effort she makes to please him. She warms his pyjamas on the electric blanket every night.

He has lost his faith but it is Kol Nidre night and the habit of ritual is strong and, after all, how can anyone be so certain? Maybe God exists. Better to be safe than sorry. Better to go to the synagogue tonight and again tomorrow. Better to fast, better to pray, better to ask for another year of life – just in case.

She is waiting for him in the lounge-room. She is wearing her fur coat. She is always cold. She even wears her coat when she sits outside, eating fruit in the sunshine. He does not know how to keep her warm.

If only that fire hadn't burned his business down. He'd planned to keep working for another six months but thieves had broken into his shop and, finding no money, they'd expressed their frustration by setting fire to the whole place. Too old to start again. Too late to rebuild.

Retirement. Strolling with her each day around the safe, known streets; letting her tell him, over and over again, the names of all the flowers and plants; walking slowly up the hill to the Scoop grocery store to buy a few cartons of yoghurt, a litre of milk. Going to the bridge club twice a week. The only thing that keeps him sane. But how much longer can he go there? She's an embarrassment. She can't remember even the last five minutes' play. The other players won't tolerate her too much longer. What will happen to him then? They've had to give up playing bridge at home. The anxiety caused by having to provide people with sandwiches and cups of tea is too great for her to bear. They buy all their meals from the gourmet food shop.

He remembers her as she used to be. Chief pharmacist of a large hospital. How proud of her he had been! He wouldn't let her work, not for a long time. Not his wife. His wife didn't need to work. After all, he earned enough money, didn't he? Enough to support her and the children – all quite comfortably. But she wouldn't give up. She pestered and begged and finally he'd let her go back to work. What a difference it had made to her! She could whip through her day with lightning precision; dash home with swift steps, feet flying; cook dinner, wash the dishes, iron clothes, help the children with their homework. Phenomenal! Her momentum propelled her through the days, the months, the years. No one could keep pace with her.

And the Friday nights, the family dinners, children and grandchildren spilling around the swimming pool. How can it have come to this? Now, now when they should be enjoying the rewards of his hard-working life. He thinks of his children. All successful, thank goodness. All well-educated. Not like him. Not reliant on the business world. And yet, he'd done well, hadn't he? Comfortably off. Not rich but comfortable. 'The whitest man in the rag trade.' That's what they called him. Too honest to be rich. And too much given away to charity, so some people would say. But isn't that the most important part of being a Jew? Doing mitzvahs – giving to those less fortunate than yourself. They could have gone on a world cruise if only she'd managed to keep hold of her mind.

He looks at her, sitting in the lounge chair, waiting for him. Frail now. So thin. Her upper lip trembles. Her gloved hands grasp her handbag very tightly. He tells her it won't be long. Soon the taxi will arrive to take them into the city.

They are walking down Elizabeth Street towards the Great Synagogue. It is 5.45 pm. He knows that the service begins at 6 pm but he has to get there early. He is a man of extreme punctuality. If he is not 15 minutes early, then he considers himself to be late.

It is difficult for him to walk quickly because the arteries in his legs no longer function properly and he suffers from angina. Her pace slows down to match his. The wind claws into her. If she did not have her fur coat on, she would surely die.

They reach the synagogue and find that the gates are closed. Not only are the gates closed, but heavy, locked chains hold the gates together.

'We must be very early,' he says to her. 'I must have mistaken the time. Perhaps the service doesn't start until 6.30 pm.'

'It's so cold, dear,' she complains. 'I can't just stand still. I'll have to keep walking.'

'Come on, then, Mummy dear, we'll walk round to the Castlereagh Street entrance. It's bound to be open.'

By the time they walk around the block to the back entrance of the synagogue, it is 6 pm. The tall, brown doors are closed and locked. The street is empty.

'Let's walk back to the front, dear,' he says. 'By the time we do that, they must be open.' He walks swiftly now and her pace quickens to keep up with him. He should slow down, he should be calm. He knows that if he gets upset this angina will get worse but his agitation is beyond control.

The front of the synagogue is still locked. He moves away from her and stares at the gates in disbelief. She pulls the collar of her coat up around her chin. 'There must be some reason, dear, why the synagogue is closed,' she says. 'I don't know what that reason could be, but there must be a reason.'

He does not hear her. Where are all his fellow Jews? Don't they know, as he does, that they must begin their fasting and their atonement on this night? Why are they so late opening the synagogue? He goes to the gates and rattles them. He pulls at the chains. His mind is mathematical, decisive and precise. He never makes mistakes about dates and times. The synagogue must be open. It must! No other possibility is tenable. He grabs the heavy iron gates and shakes, shakes, shakes them. 'Open the gates!' he cries. 'Open the gates and let me in! God, let me in! Put my name, my name … down – my name, write my name in the Book of Life!'

She stands apart from him, waiting, whipped by the wind. She folds her hands into the sleeves of her coat.

He stops, lets the gates go. His hands drop, head sags. He stares at her in blank confusion and a tear spills out of the corner of his eye. He takes her arm and they lean against each other, tightening themselves against the wind, shuffling through the darkness, along deserted Elizabeth Street.

NURSING HOME

(Published in the Weekend Australian newspaper – 1987)

They tie my mother into a chair. At mealtimes. To restrain her. Otherwise she would get up and walk out of the nursing home dining room. She would wander around the confusing corridors, looking for room 146. Mealtimes are for eating. The nurses don't want befuddled old ladies getting lost at mealtimes. Understandable. No matter if she has forgotten what mealtimes are for. No matter if her body tells her that there is no need to eat. Not matter if she, always so slim, has put on at least six kilograms of unnecessary weight. Institutions cannot cater for individuals.

I'm just as bad as they are. I bring her yoghurt and licorice, nuts and fruit. I bring her 4711 Ice Cologne. I buy her a box of pink Kleenex tissues every week. She takes out each tissue and folds it into a small square and piles the squares one on top of the other on her bedside cabinet. Every week she tells me I shouldn't spend my money buying her these things, and every week I have to tell her that the money for the little extras she needs does not come out my pocket. It comes from her own considerable investments. It's just that I'm the person in the family who has taken on the responsibility of buying the yoghurt and the fruit, the tissues and the toothpaste. She does not understand. She is so considerate, so polite, so worried that she is taking up my time, my energy, my money.

I visit her twice a week. I take her for walks around the streets near the nursing home. Every time I see her, I am darkened by guilt – that I do not see her more often, that I do not take her out. I used to bring her home to my place once a fortnight. On a Sunday. For lunch. But I've given up. Rational conversation is impossible. My children find it depressing trying to communicate with her. And yet I know she loved to come. Just to see the children. Just to watch them. She didn't even ask to participate. The children want to remember her as she was — their real grandmother — active, lively, intelligent. It is worse than tragic. It evokes in me a hollowness beyond tears.

So I visit her twice a week. I make these visits on the basis of what my beloved father would have expected of me, had he been alive. To do the best I can, without destroying myself.

I take her for walks when I visit her. If it is raining on a day that I am to visit her, I am filled with despair. I cannot tolerate being cosseted with her in her room, so, if it's raining, I tell her I've just called in quickly on my way to work. I tell her that, even if it's a Sunday. Days and dates mean nothing to her.

When we walk around the streets, she tells me the names of the flowers and asks me, endlessly, 'How are the boys? How is that little girl of yours, the one who cooks?' I murmur, 'Fine. Very well.' It is no good trying to initiate conversation. It is only possible to respond.

She always has a lot to tell me when we go on our walks. She tells me that my unmarried, 78-year-old aunt is pregnant; that the upper floor of the nursing home is a gambling casino; that my brother has a girlfriend whom he keeps in the room next to hers (she can hear his voice when he comes to visit the lady). No matter what I am wearing, even if I am attired in my oldest clothes, she always tells me how pretty I look. She particularly likes my blue sandals. She greets everyone we meet in the corridors with absolute politeness. She says, 'Good afternoon' at 10 o'clock in the morning and 'Good morning' at 3 o'clock in the afternoon. She always introduces me, sometimes as her sister, sometimes as her daughter. The sisters and nurses treat her with great tenderness, for which I am grateful. 'She's a beautiful lady, your mother,' they say to me. And so she is.

As we walk along the streets, she talking, me responding, I start to feel quite peaceful. Her endless delight in the gardens, the trees, the houses, the flowers, the plants seems enough. We stop at the corner store for and ice-cream.

Then we start to walk back. As we near the nursing home, she will say, 'Now, where was I before I was here?' It is not a philosophical question. It is a geographical question. I tell her, 'Remember, you were in your room when I came. You were sitting in your chair by the window having a little rest when I arrived. And then we came out to have a walk.'

'Well, I've never been in a place like this. How will I find my way?'

'Don't worry, Mum,' I reassure her. 'I'll take you back to your room.'

We wait for the lift. She reads the sign every time. 'In case of fire, do not use lift.' The lift is slow in arriving, and I can feel her anxiety. She does not know where she is. We go up to Level 1 and get out of the lift and walk along the corridor until we come to room 146. She is momentarily reassured by the fact that her name is printed clearly above the room number.

I take her inside. 'See, Mum, this is your room. Look at your photos, your clock, your shawl, your clothes.'

'Is there a bathroom here?' she asks. 'I'd like to pass water.' Her room is like a motel unit. It is tasteful, modern, bright. She has her own fridge, her own TV, her own bathroom. I show her where the bathroom is. Sometimes she knows how to use the toilet; sometimes she doesn't. She needs help in readjusting her petticoat and skirt.

She comes out of the bathroom. This is the time I dread. I want to make my escape. 'What do you feel like doing?' she asks, always solicitous. 'I have to get home and make dinner for the children,' I say, or, 'I have to do the ironing,' or, 'I have to go to work.'

Her upper lip begins to tremble. 'That's just it, you see, I don't know what to do here. What happens next?'

'Don't worry,' I assure her, 'the nurses will come and get you when it's time for lunch.' I can see from her face that what I'm saying to her is quite meaningless. She lives in a lost world. Let her be brave! Let her hold onto herself! Don't let her cry before I leave the room!

'I have to go now, Mum,' I say, kissing her, pretending there is nothing wrong. 'I'll see you in a few days' time.'

I can't look into her face. I rush out of her room and close the door. I walk down the corridor as quickly as I can, just in case she opens her door and comes after me. The lift takes an eternity to come. Eventually I get out of the building and into my car. And drive away, away from her emptiness, from her loneliness, and I cannot wait to immerse myself in the child-warmth and chaos and the disordered vitality of my home.

We took her out on Christmas Day. We all went to my sister's house at Pearl Beach. My brother drove her up there. There were 24 of us, sitting around a long table, out on the verandah, just above the beach. I put a home-baked bread roll on her plate, with the turkey and salads. She didn't know what to do with it. She tried to cut it up with her knife and fork.

After lunch, we took her for a swim. She always loved the water. She put on her bathing cap and took off with a slow, smooth breast-stroke. She swam and swam. We felt pleased that she was enjoying herself. Suddenly, she started to change direction. She began to swim out to sea; swift, strong, sure. We called to her, 'Mum! Mum! Don't go out so far!' We called, her children, trying to protect her. She didn't hear us. My brother had to swim out and grab hold of her and bring her back.

If we were still a tribe, she would have wandered off by now. She would have walked out into the desert or got lost in a blizzard or swum out to sea. But we look after her. We keep her in expensive safety. They are infinitely kind to her at the nursing home, so how can I complain if they judge it necessary to tie my mother into a chair at mealtimes?

BENEVOLENT PATRIARCH

An essay about my father.

(Published in Fathers in Writing – Tuart House – University of Western Australia
Press – 1997)

My father, Sid Sperling, was born in Poland in 1900 in a town called Nowy Sacz about three hours' drive out of Krakow. I went there in 1994 because I wanted to know what it would feel like to visit the place where he was born. On the wall of the synagogue was a plaque which said: '25,000 Jews lived in this town before World War II. All of them died in concentration camps.' Not one Jew remains in Nowy Sacz. Most Jewish families have tragic stories to recount of despair and death and destruction but my family has no such tale to tell. The members of my family were not victims. They were survivors.

This seems to me to be the right place to begin an essay on my father because the actions of my grandfather, Leo Sperling, determined the kind of life my father had to lead and there is no doubt in my mind that my father's way of life and his attitudes were primary influences in shaping the course of my own life.

My grandfather, Leo, one of seven brothers and six sisters, was a career officer in the Austrian army and was stationed at Nowy Sacz at the time of my father's birth. There were many young Jewish men in the town who did not want to do their military service and my grandfather, from his position of influence within the army, quietly worked to help them avoid such an unpleasant prospect. The family story goes that my grandmother, who was only seventeen years old at the time, boasted about her husband's subversive activities; the army hierarchy found out what he was doing and, in 1901, the family was forced to leave Nowy Sacz in a great hurry to avoid punishment. The story is also told that my grandfather donned female apparel to effect his escape.

They fled to America. In 1995 I visited the Immigration Centre on Ellis Island in New York and was deeply moved by the experience. I knew my family must have come through here. How did he feel, my grandfather, at the prospect of a new life in a new world? Twenty-six years old, unable to speak English, trained only for the army, burdened by the responsibility of a young wife and a one-year-old son. They went to Chicago. By lying about his work experience, Leo got a job as a cutter in a clothing factory. The story goes that he was thrown out after one day but had managed to pick up a few skills. The next job lasted two days. The next a week. Gradually he learned all aspects of the rag trade. Several of Leo's brothers and sisters followed him to America and settled in Chicago. A few of his brothers died young but out of all those thirteen siblings only one sister, who was blind, perished in the Holocaust.

For some reason my grandfather became dissatisfied with life in Chicago and moved his family to Vancouver. By that time two more children had been born, my Aunt Betti and my Uncle Sam. In 1909, when my father was nine years old, a terrible accident occurred; it was to change the course of my family's history.

Five-year-old Sam was run over by a truck. One of his legs was badly crushed. According to family mythology, the bones were shattered so badly that they had to be strung together with gold wire. As a child, whenever this story was told to me, the image of bones sewn together by golden thread always seemed so magical that it took my breath away. There was insufficient

skin to cover the horrendous wounds and, in a double opera-
tion, skin was cut from my grandfather's stomach and grafted
onto his son's leg. This event was newsworthy. It was one of the
first person-to-person skin grafts ever performed and it made
the headlines in the daily newspapers.

Sam made a good recovery, although he was left with a slight
limp for life, but my grandfather did not do so well. The wound
on his stomach became infected, septicaemia set in, he had to
take weeks off from work. It was bitterly cold in Vancouver and
the doctor told Leo that he must move to a warmer climate
if he wanted to recover his health. Los Angeles was suggested
but my grandfather told the doctor that he had a young family
to protect; he would not run the risk of moving them to an
earthquake-prone city.

One day when he was, no doubt, feeling depressed and
despondent about his situation, my grandfather went to a news-
reel theatre and saw a film clip depicting the American fleet's
arrival in Sydney Harbour. There it was! Warmth! Sunshine!
Surely his precious family would be safe in such a paradise. He
rushed home and told his wife that he was going to Australia.

The only problem was that he did not have enough money
for his boat ticket. Nevertheless, in the Jewish way of life, family
loyalty is so strong and the obligation to help a fellow Jew so
great that he was sure he could borrow the money for his
fare to Australia. My father, aged nine, was entrusted with the
task of going to collect the money. An uncle was working as a
lumberjack in a timber camp up in the north of Canada and
my father was put on a steamship with a note for his uncle. The
journey took four or five days. I think of that little boy who
was to become my father and I wonder what it was like for
him. Was he afraid to travel alone? Did he feel overwhelmed

by the weight of the burden of responsibility that had been placed on him? Or is the fact that my grandfather had absolute faith in his son's ability to carry out such an undertaking simply an example of how much the world has changed? Could any of my three sons, at the age if nine have done what my father had to do?

When my father arrived at the lumber camp, he was warmly welcomed and his one night's stay with his uncle left an indelible impression. He was given buckwheat pancakes to eat, with maple syrup, and the memory of the taste of those pancakes remained with him forever. At regular intervals he would ask my mother to cook him buckwheat pancakes with maple syrup and although he appreciated her efforts, it was obvious from his nostalgic sighs that nothing could match the original experience. The money my grandfather had asked for was tied into a bandage around my father's waist before he boarded the steamer for his journey back to Vancouver.

My grandfather went alone to Australia. His aim was to work hard and bring his family out as soon as he had enough money to do so. He arrived in Sydney at 6 am on a Friday morning, disembarked, bought a copy of the Sydney Morning Herald and by 7 am was sitting outside a clothing factory that had advertised for a cutter. When the proprietor arrived he said to my grandfather, 'How long have you been here?'

'Two hours,' my grandfather replied.

'No, I don't mean how long you've been waiting here; I mean how long have you been in Australia?'

'Two hours,' repeated my grandfather.

Needless to say, he gave my grandfather the job. In less than a year the rest of the family were safely in Australia.

I don't know how my grandmother and her three children survived without my grandfather but I've no doubt that relatives, or other member of the Jewish community, supported them financially during that time. I imagine that the sense of family responsibility that ruled my grandfather's life was by now so ingrained in my father that he must have provided his mother, his sister and his brother with unstinting solace and support despite the fact that he was only ten years old at the time of his arrival in Australia.

I understand now that my father lived in a prison defined by his parents' values. My grandparents were not assimilated into the broad Australian community. They chose to live within the folds of a very narrow-minded, self-imposed ghetto of Sydney Jewish culture. All social contact was Jewish and a Jew who became friends with a non-Jew was considered a pariah by my ignorant and prejudiced grandmother. My grandfather was more tolerant but he chose the hypocritical path of agreeing with my grandmother's views for the sake of family peace.

My grandfather established a women's clothing factory in a building at the railway end of Castlereagh Street and everyone had to work very hard to make the business successful. My father, his sister and his brother had no career choices. They had to leave school at fourteen and join the family business. My father worked at cutting and pressing, my Aunt Betti learned how to design the clothes and my Uncle Sam looked after dispatch. Every aspect of my father's life was determined by family obligation.

The business expanded from wholesale manufacture to include retail selling and a Sperling Frock Shop was opened in Newcastle. My father was sent there to manage the shop. At the age of twenty-three, while living in Newcastle, he committed the ultimate act of family betrayal – he married a woman who was not Jewish. A cocoon of silence was spun around my father's first marriage and I knew nothing about it until I was thirty years old. It was then that my brother, who had been entrusted with the shameful secret at the age of thirteen, finally decided to share his knowledge with my sister and me. I thought at first that my father's 'marrying out' was a gesture of rebellion and defiance, but that was not so. The woman was older than my father and had pretended to be pregnant to trap him into what proved to be a very short, very painful marriage. He must have considered my brother's barmitzvah a suitable time for imparting a dire warning on the dangers of marrying out of the faith. My brother was sworn to secrecy and I, in turn, had to promise I would never let my father know that I knew his secret.

The knowledge of my father's first marriage provided the key to understanding many aspects of his behaviour which I had resented and felt angry about when I was growing up. In many ways my father was a hypocrite and I felt this hypocrisy keenly without ever understanding its cause. I hated it so deeply that I was determined never to be like him in this respect. I would live a life of truth and honesty, not hide behind a false, superficial, conventional façade.

My father was a good man. No-one could find any fault with his behaviour. He was so honest that he was known as the whitest man in the rag trade. He was a pillar of the Jewish community. He belonged to the Board of Deputies of the Great Synagogue. He was a patron of the Great Synagogue Youth. He was a mason, belonging to both the Grand Masonic Lodge and Lodge Mark Owen. And yet I sensed always that there was an element of insincerity in his devotion to duty and good works, that he did not fully believe in the causes to which he devoted so much of his time.

He was not really an orthodox Jew. We did not eat kosher food. He never gave me the impression of holding a devout belief in God, yet he certainly believed in maintaining the appearance of being a religious man. We had to park the car miles away from the Great Synagogue on a Saturday morning so that it looked as if we had walked to the service, all the way from Dover Heights. We had to attend Sunday school and additional religious instruction classes on Tuesday and Thursday afternoons. I hated all this but I don't recall rebelling against it. I simply accepted that this was the way Jewish people lived their lives. My rebellion occurred later, when I became a committed atheist and rejected entirely the Jewish community that had enclosed me as a child.

I resented the time my father spent on the Jewish community because it limited the time he could spend with us. And he gave us such good times – teaching me to swim at Bondi Beach; barbecue picnics at the royal National Park, where he taught me how to row a boat and paddle a canoe. Life had been so real and earnest for him as a child that he encouraged us to enjoy ourselves as much as possible. Our friends were always welcome and on Friday nights our house was open to old friends, new friends, or to anyone else who seemed to be in need of a meal. When we reached our teenage years he had a large terrace at the side of the house converted into a room with a parquet floor, suitable for dancing. We were allowed to have as many parties as we pleased. He believed in spending money, not saving it, but he did not spend all his money on us. He saw it as his duty to help anyone who was less fortunate than himself. He always looked for the good in people and seemed to be oblivious to their faults. I used to think he walked through life with blinkers on but I realize now that he was, quite simply, the most tolerant man I've ever known.

I also resented the time he spent with my grandmother. He built her a house a few hundred yards away from ours and he visited her constantly. In his devotion to her, I sensed that same element of hypocrisy. She was an awful woman. He may have loved her but she was so nasty, so possessive and so demanding that he must also have hated her; yet he waited upon her from the time of my grandfather's death in 1936 until her own death twenty-seven years later.

Learning of my father's first marriage made the hypocrisy of his behaviour understandable to me. He had spent a lifetime in expiation. He was paying for the sin of 'marrying out' by serving the Jewish community and by dancing attendance upon my grandmother. My father was sixty-five years old when his mother died and his liberation was a joy to witness. He resigned from all his Jewish committees and although he continued to run a business until he was eight-one years old, all his spare time was devoted to his children and grandchildren.

My father did not want his children to be trapped within the suffocating bonds of family responsibility as he had been. He wanted us to be educated and he wanted us to be free. In fact, he made it quite clear that none of us would be permitted to enter the family business. We all had to go to university. My father was unusual in this belief that his daughters, as well as his son, must be educated. There is no doubt that my mother's influence helped him to formulate this viewpoint. She was a hospital pharmacist and he was very proud of her education and her intelligence although he did not allow her to go back to work until we had all completed high school.

So my father wanted me to be educated and liberated but did he really like the results? He must have disapproved of the fact that I insisted on being truthful and honest in my words and deeds even when my truthfulness hurt others. Here was a daughter who was an atheist, believed in free love, swam at nudist beaches and wore Indian clothes. And yet I know that part of him envied me. When I discussed my atheistic beliefs with him he told me that I must be a much stronger person than he was, that he would not have had the courage to live without a belief in God. He probably disapproved of my nude swimming, yet he jokingly offered to pay the fine should I be arrested. After my divorce, I changed lovers so frequently that he must have been shocked to the core, but the closest he ever came to criticism was a gentle warning that I should not a allow one particularly irresponsible lover of mine to drive my car while my children were in it.

And how hurt was he when my insistence that I must live my life according to my own truth meant that his precious grandsons did not undergo ritual circumcision? I did have them circumcised but this was done in Crown Street Hospital, by my gynaecologist, under sterile conditions. And then, as a confirmed atheist, I could not allow my children to attend synagogue or Sunday school. Barmitzvahs were out of the question. My children had to be like me – brave and strong and independent. No religious crutches for them. They must learn to rely only upon themselves.

He must have disapproved of my divorce, of the free and open household I set up, of the way I brought up my children – permitting them to swear, dressing them in hippie clothes, allowing the boys to have long hair, sending them to a pro-gressive school. I did everything that was humanly possible to encourage my children to be individuals, to question society, to distrust conformity.

And how did my father react to all this? Not with criticism but with love. After my divorce, he gave me constant physical, financial and emotional support. He bought me new cars, refrigerators, washing machines and clothes driers. He paid the children's fees at the progressive school. He bought all their clothes and shoes. Every school holiday he gave me two hundred dollars to spend on outings and every Christmas holidays he paid to take us all away to Ettalong for a week. My parents picked the children up from school two days a week, and provided them with dinner, so that my teaching time-table would be easier for me to manage. The children spent every Saturday at his house, swimming in the pool in the summer and being taken out to parks and playgrounds in the winter. He was so generous, so good, so loving and so kind that I could weep at the thought of the pain my prolonged rebellion must have caused him.

And yet, beneath that love and generosity there did lie disapproval. And because that disapproval was so basic, because it was directed at my lifestyle, at the very essence of my personality, I must ask myself what effect it has on a daughter to live forever with the silent, subtle, underlying disapproval of a father she respected and loved. Is this the cause of a nagging dissatisfaction with myself and my achievements? Is my disapproval of myself really a reflection of his unspoken, unexpressed disapproval of me?

My father taught me the full meaning of unconditional love and his example lives through me in the uncritical and unconditional love that I have always been able to bestow upon my four children. And his benign patriarchy also lives through me. When I became a single parent I turned into a matriarch. But it was not my mother's role that I followed. My power and my strength as head of my family came from following my father's model. Even now, thirteen years after his death, I ask myself what my father would have done and how he would have reacted to any particular family situation. This remains the guide to my own behaviour.

My father loved all his three children but even my brother and my sister would agree that his love for me bordered on obsession. He adored me and I found his adoration bewildering and terrifying. I was afraid to be alone with my father. He would never have touched me in any sexual way, yet I am sure the unconscious feeling that he might was the basis of my fear. Once I had reached puberty I did everything I could to avoid ever being touched by him and if he kissed me, as of course he sometimes did, my whole body would tense in revulsion. This fear was felt most keenly when I was alone in the car with him. Naturally he was the kind of father who insisted on dropping and picking up his daughters at night rather than allowing them to take public transport. At such times my feeling of being trapped was so intense that I found it difficult to stop myself from screaming. It was not until after I had children of my own that I was able to be physically comfortable with him. I felt for my children that same overwhelming, passionate, obsessive love that he obviously had felt for me. I was, at last, able to understand and forgive.

Being the object of a father's obsessive love has its consequences for a daughter. In my relationships with men I have always sought obsessive adoration and then responded by feeling trapped by the very thing I craved. My father's love for me and my love for him have somehow made it impossible for me to love any man successfully. I have come to the conclusion that, for me, love is something that I feel only for my children and grandchildren.

Although my father adored me, he saw my career choices as inferior to my brother's. The fact that he had a son who was first a barrister and then a successful Queen's Counsel was the primary source of his pride as a father. My teaching and writing were certainly acknowledged. And he admired the way my sister carved out for herself such an interesting and varied working life. But, in his estimation, our achievements fell far short of our brother's. Our real value lay in the wonderful grandchildren we had produced. My sister even provided him with great-grandchildren.

My mother would not let him read my first novel, Coins for the Ferryman, on the grounds that it would upset him. I acquiesced in her decision because, as a daughter, I was uncomfortable to think of him reading those parts of the book that dealt with my journey of sexual exploration. He was, however, sufficiently proud of me to take copies of the book to Israel and present them to his relatives there. Before he died I had completed the first part of Mother's Day and gave it to him to read. Although this writing must have shocked him profoundly, he paid me the compliment of telling me that he'd had no idea that I could write so powerfully.

In January 1995, my brother became a judge of the New South Wales Supreme Court. My father's spirit hovered in the courtroom during the swearing-in ceremony. Almost every member of the family was there and I am certain that each of us saw this day as the culmination of the meaning of my father's life.

Sid Sperling. Benevolent patriarch. Beloved father. I am absolutely at peace with you.

FOUR LEAF CLOVER

(Published in the Sun-Herald in 1984 – a time when the threat of nuclear war was very real.)

Today I went on the anti-nuclear march with my children. As it was the first time that I had ever participated in such a demonstration, I expected to be exalted by the experience. I was not.

Instead of exhilaration, I was assailed by a sense of parental guilt, a feeling that I had brought four children into a world without a future.

I do not read the news. I do not listen to the news. My refusal to look at the state of the world around me has been quite deliberate. I have felt that the only way I could bring my children up to believe that life was good and beautiful was by denying the state of the world around me.

Yet here I was, sitting on the hill in the Domain, being told by Dr Caldicott exactly what I could expect to happen to my children and my world if a nuclear war occurred and being told, moreover, how perilously close we were to such an event.

I left the rally very depressed, feeling that neither her voice nor mine, nor the voices of the 150,000 people present at the rally would ever have the power to allay a nuclear holocaust.

That certainty of world destruction called into question the whole of my parental philosophy. What right did I have to encourage my children to study, to be diligent, to plan for a future when I felt reasonably certain that they were not going to have a future?

And what was the point of what I was doing? Why bother to teach, to write, to be an effective parent? Why bother about anything?

My 18-year-old was left wondering why he was making the effort to go to university and expressed the view that he was glad that at least he had seen half of the world.

My 15-year-old said that the rally made him feel that if he was going to be blown up, then there was not much point in trying to achieve anything.

It was my 16-year-old, however, who saved me from despair. He came back from the rally in a state of euphoria.

Of Dr Caldicott's speech he said this, 'You only have to hear a message like that once. You know that what she is saying is the truth. You have to listen and then you have to forget it. Otherwise you can't live your life. But you have to remember it, too. You have to go to rallies. You have to march, but you have to live your life as if there is a future.'

Even if the anti-nuclear rally achieves nothing in a practical sense, it was a grand and magnificent gesture, a demonstration to us all that the human spirit is defiant and indomitable.

I forgot to mention that the only way my 12-year-old could cope with Dr Calciott's message was by completely blocking it out of her mind.

During the speech she found two four-leaved clovers in less than five minutes. I've looked for four-leaved clovers all my life but never found one.

She left the rally with an absolute faith in her own good luck. Perhaps it was a sign that she will be lucky enough to survive the destruction of the world.

THE MAY SCHOOL HOLIDAYS

(Published in the Sun-Herald in 1984, when the video-recorder was a new, exciting form of home entertainment.)

The prospect of coping with the May school holidays has always haunted me, partly because the weather seems so bleak.

I have two sons with birthdays in May and when they were smaller I used to pray that winter would not begin before their birthday parties were over. How could one tolerate 12 or 15 little boys inside the house!

My prayers were never answered. I can tell you with absolute certainty that winter always begins during the May school holidays.

At first I used to think that I was alone in being unable to handle them. As I dragged my four children through the Zoo, Paradise Gardens, the Lion Safari, Adventureland and whatever other places existed for family enjoyment, I wondered why I was quite incapable of enjoying myself.

The only outings I actually enjoyed were taking them to the movies. There I could sink into the darkness. Nothing was demanded of me. I did not have to join in any activities. We saw a lot of movies.

I used to think that my inadequacy was due to being a single parent. I have since realized that most mothers are single parents during the May school holidays, unless, of course, they happen to be married to school teachers.

Once I hired a caravan at Katoomba for a week during the May holidays. I was determined that we would have a healthy holiday tramping up and down mountains. However, three of them were still wetting the bed and I seemed to spend all day at the local automatic laundry, washing and drying the sleeping bags.

Now, of course, they are much bigger and I am not really required to provide them with entertainment. However, a household containing four teenagers can soon disintegrate into endless conflict if no outlets are provided for them.

This year the idea of the May holidays loomed somewhat despairingly on my horizon. This is largely because I don't have much money. It costs $30 to take them to the movies by the time you buy the Maltesers and Choctops at interval. It costs $40 to take them to a Chinese restaurant, perhaps $60 to go to the theatre. They love all these pleasurable and civilized activities. Who doesn't?

This year, however, I came up with the perfect solution. I hired a video-recorder. They all agreed to give up drinking Coca-Cola and the money thus saved was to pay for hiring the video machine.

Hiring a video-recorder was not expensive. We were prepared to buy one instead of hiring one but then, as the kids kept reminding me, we were comparing the cost of hiring a video machine with the cost of Coca-Cola.

We were not concerned with the comparative costs of hiring and buying. The video companies with whom I talked had some difficulty in understanding my frame of reference.

We were also pressured to join extraordinary video-library borrowing schemes. The cost? - $250 to belong to a library for life! And then it would only cost $2 a film on top of that – forever! The young man was very persistent and did not seem to be programmed to find an answer to my suggestion that we might all be dead in a year's time.

I found joining a local video-library very easy and very reasonable - $100 for 50 movies. I thought that was good value. I have hired the machine for a year and, at one movie a week, I thought it a good investment.

I must say that I have a great resistance to the electronic age. I steadfastly refuse to be seduced by computer developments. I'm the last of the book readers. I don't watch television and I refuse to have a Handybank card. I felt, therefore, something of a traitor to my ideals in hiring a contraption that would hold my children for even more hours to the television screen in our lounge-room.

It is now the end of the first week of the holidays and they and I are completely seduced. We wallow in our own personal film festival. We devour film after film, taking a little time for light refreshments in between.

I keep trying to resist. I try to avoid the lounge-room but it's right next to the kitchen. What can I do when I see Merry Christmas Mr Lawrence flickering across the screen? How can I resist Garp and Roberta? What willpower can I call upon when Woody Allen takes over? So we all curl up in sleeping bags and eiderdowns. We all sink comfortable into the velvet beanbags and allow ourselves to be whisked away by motion picture magic.

And why not? The only problem is that it's counter productive. I keep telling them that next week we all have to spring clean the house, study for school exams, do our projects, write some poetry, perhaps even begin writing another novel. 'Yes, yes,' they reply.

At our present rate of film consumption, my $100 investment in 50 movies will be well and truly used up by the end of the May holidays.

I have to stop writing now because they're calling out to me that Sophie's Choice is about to begin. I can't miss out on that, now can I?

Just before I go, I must say that this whole exercise does have some positive value. Sibling rivalry is at a lower level. There is no Coca-Cola in the house. And, yes, I'm drinking decaffinated coffee. If they could give up their addiction, it seemed only fair that I should give up mine.

PRONE TO EXAGGERATION

(Published in the Sun-Herald in 1984)

I am 'prone to exaggeration'. That's what it says in the palmistry book I recently bought for my 15-year-old son.

He is very excited about his new book and keeps running to check my palms to see if the lines bear out accurately what he knows to be true of my life.

The lines show many things that I am only too happy to accept as truths; that I am intelligent, that I am creative, that I am independent, that I place my children ahead of my relationships – there's even a clearly defined asterisk beneath the fourth finger on my right palm that my son interprets as the achievement of literary acclaim in my own lifetime.

If I want to believe all these things (and I certainly do) then I must also accept that 'a strong sloping headline terminating in a fork suggests that the subject is prone to exaggeration'.

'Do I exaggerate?' I ask them, innocently, expecting denial.

'Of course you do!' they reply and tumble out endless examples of my gross exaggerations.

'Remember you told us that the apples and oranges in Greece were this big,' (indicating with their hands a size approximate to that of a basketball). Well, perhaps I did exaggerate a little but when I went to Greece the fruit was enormous. However, when I took the children there, we only ever found normal-sized fruit.

In fact, at the end of the single-handed, seven-week, epic journey I took through Europe with my four children, they told me that the only things I had not exaggerated were the beauty of Delphi and the size of Michelangelo's David.

Then they tell me that whenever I'm recounting something that has happened, I exaggerate it. Surely, however, the truth is more interesting if you embroider it just a little. Exaggeration? No! Poetic licence, I'd call it.

The children also tell me that I have exaggerated reactions to perfectly normal occurrences. For example, when they roll around the lounge-room floor, shouting, screaming, wrestling and clawing, I think they are killing each other whereas they assure me that they are just having fun.

There is, however, one area in which I must admit to the character trait of exaggeration. I have exaggerated fears concerning the possible fate of those I love.

I think I inherited this trait from my father. My father taught me an absolute precision about time. He believed that if you were not five minutes early, then you were late. If ever I were late arriving at his house, he would ring up to find out where I was. He was not angry at my being late; he rang because he believed that I had been killed on the way from Ryde to Lindfield – a reasonably safe route by any standards.

I have the same exaggerated fears for my children. I remember that my first independent act, as a single parent, was to take my children, then aged three, five, seven and nine to Bondi Beach for the day.

As they all rushed into the water, I was assailed by the most powerful sense of panic as I realized that I could not possibly watch them all at once. I decided that I would have to keep my eyes on the youngest and stoically accepted the fact that the other three were going to drown.

I am sure that I am not alone in conjuring up horrific pictures of what might have happened to my children if they are late home. They might have been run over, kidnapped, murdered, raped. There are mothers and fathers all over Sydney who lie awake, thinking such thoughts, until their children are safely home.

My oldest son is just nineteen. I've stopped worrying about him. He has been driving my car for two years, doesn't drink, has never had an accident. He is mature and responsible. I trust him absolutely.

He goes out at least two nights a week to listen to music at various places around Sydney and I don't stay awake any longer waiting for him to come home.

A few nights ago, my son went to Sans Souci to listen to a favourite band. When he got into the car to return home, he was attacked by three drunken youths carrying crowbars.

They banged on the car and demanded that my son get out and fight them. My son and his two friends had done nothing to provoke this violence and they stayed inside the car. They were trapped. There was nothing they could do but stay calm and hope for the best.

They were saved by the fact that a nearby car caught fire. This momentarily distracted the attackers and my son was able to make a swift getaway with the car damaged but himself unhurt.

If, as the palmistry book says, I am 'prone to exaggeration', then what exaggerated fears will whirl through my mind the next time my gentle, non-aggressive son goes out to listen to music?

Perhaps even the grossest imaginings cannot match the awfulness of truth.

PAUL AND THE ELECTRIC GUITAR

Paul was a musician. Although he was only sixteen years old, Paul had been writing songs since he was eight. The trouble with Paul's songwriting was that most of it had taken place inside his head. That's because his mother didn't know he was a musician and, until a year or so ago, he'd had no musical instrument to play. Then the family inherited a piano. A week after Paul began piano lessons he started composing his own songs. His mother felt guilty then. She's had no idea about this.

Piano lessons were pretty frustrating. Paul's traditional, conventional, music teacher expected him to read the music as he played for her. The trouble was that, after hearing a tune once, he could play it and so he used to pretend to be playing from the music, whereas he was really playing by ear.

When he turned sixteen he got a cheap guitar and taught himself to play. Now songwriting began in earnest. Soon the cheap guitar seemed unsatisfactory and what Paul longed for was an electric guitar.

There was a new music shop opening at Crow's Nest. Paul heard that they were giving away two electric guitars, for $10 each, to the first two people who were there when the shop opened on the following Monday morning.

Paul told his mother that he was going to wait outside the shop all night so that he could get one of the guitars. She told him he was mad. It was mid-winter. He'd freeze to death and, anyway, he'd never get the guitar. Things like that were like winning the lottery. Things like that only happened to other people.

Paul said he was going anyway and, moreover, he said that he was going to get one of those guitars so his mother hunted around the house for woolly gloves and scarves and a heavy coat and a knitted hat and she found an old thermos in the bottom of a kitchen cupboard. She made him chicken soup and thick sandwiches and gave him a few packets of biscuits and a bag full of fruit.

A friend of Paul's, who had a car, wanted the other electric guitar and the two of them set off at about 4pm on the Sunday afternoon. The music shop was due to open at 9am the next day.

They were the first to arrive and they sat in the doorway of the shop to wait for morning. It was pretty cold, sitting there, so they decided to take turns warming up in the car. One boy minded their place and one boy sat in the car. Sometimes they sat together, in the doorway, chatting. They ate the food Paul's mother had packed for him. At 9pm the other boy went and bought them a take-away Chinese meal.

At midnight, the proprietor of the shop arrived. He was amazed to find two boys camped in his doorway.

'Do you two want to come in and help me set up?' he asked.

'Right,' said the boys, and in they went. It took about an hour to set up and the shop owner let them play the pianos and try out the guitars.

'I know you two were here first,' he said. 'If people rush in tomorrow morning, don't you worry. You two'll get the guitars. Sorry I can't let you stay inside the shop, though. I've got to go home and get some sleep.'

'That's O.K.,' said Paul, 'we'll be right.'

By now it was after 1am and bitterly cold. The shop was on a corner and the wind swept right through their clothes. The boy who owned the car was getting a bit sick of all this, even though he wanted the guitar.

'I'm going to sleep in the car,' he announced.

'Righto,' said Paul. What else could he say? After all, the car did belong to the other boy and he couldn't very well complain.

So Paul settled down in the doorway and tried to get some sleep. He was awakened by a torch shining in his face. A large, uniformed policeman loomed above him.

'What are you doing here? You can't sleep in doorways. You ought to be home in bed. It's three o'clock in the morning.'

Paul explained and the policeman said, 'O.K., but I don't like it. I could arrest you, y' know. Y' must be mad, sleeping out here on a night like this.' People didn't seem to understand how badly Paul wanted an electric guitar.

Paul couldn't sleep much and his bum ached and his fingers were numb and it was agony holding onto his piss until the other boy came to see how Paul was doing and he was able to go round the corner and pee in the gutter.

At about 6am other people began to arrive but Paul felt safe. He knew the guitar was his. When the shop opened at 9am he bought the guitar and the other boy bought his and they drove home. He couldn't go to school that day. He crawled into bed and slept for hours.

When his mother got home from work she could see the guitar in the lounge-room. She couldn't believe her eyes. She hugged Paul and said she was glad but she said she still thought he was mad to even think of queuing up like that, not knowing whether he'd get the guitar or not.

'But I did know,' he said. 'I dreamed it, weeks ago. I dreamed about the shop and the man who let us in. He looked exactly the same as in my dream. A small bloke with a thinnish face and a little pointed beard. And I dreamed the part about him letting us into the shop as well. I knew for certain I'd get that guitar. All I had to do was be there.'

Paul's mother did not want to believe all this because she was a total pragmatist and stories like this were alien to her understanding of the universe. 'Don't be silly,' she said.

'I've dreamed other things before this, things that have come true but I don't tell you about them because I don't think you'll believe me.'

A few months later, Paul's cousin was diagnosed with a possible brain tumour. All the family feared that she was going to die. When Paul heard the news he was shocked and went downstairs to play the piano to calm himself. He concentrated very hard on his cousin. He put all his thoughts and all his love into her. The door to the backyard was open and suddenly a shaft of golden light bolted through the sky and momentarily blinded him.

He came upstairs to tell his mother. 'It's alright,' he said. 'She isn't going to die,' and he explained why he knew this to be true. His mother, sceptic that she was, treated this information as a piece of wishful thinking.

Paul was right, of course. His cousin made a complete recovery and Paul's mother was forced, reluctantly, to think that there had been something both strange and wonderful in the way that Paul had become the owner of an electric guitar.

APPROVAL

(Publish in the Sydney Morning Herald newspaper – 1988)

'We are all looking into each other's eyes, seeking approval.' That's what he said to me, one day, after he'd finished making love to me. We were sitting on his bed, drinking tea.

'And you,' I said, 'is that true for you too?'

'Goodness me,' he replied, 'I don't count. I'm just a robot, a recycled washing machine.'

Afterwards I thought about what he'd said. I remembered when my oldest son came back from overseas. His girlfriend had come over to our house to stay the night so that she could come with us, early in the morning, to meet him at the airport. She was nervous about his return. She brought bunches of roses to put in his room. She even brought her own portable television set with her so that she could watch it all night. She knew she wouldn't be able to sleep.

She set her hair and manicured her nails. She got up at 5 am to bathe and dress. She wore a black and white outfit with a tight, low-cut bodice and a wide, full skirt. She looked as if she were going to a cocktail party. She wore eye-shadow and mascara and eye-liner so that her already huge black eyes started out of her skull. Large, liquid eyes, longing for approval. When I saw her I wanted to cry. I wanted to warn her. I wanted to remind her how much my son hates make-up. I wanted to tell her that no one goes out to the airport to meet an 8 am plane looking like that. But I kept quiet. None of my business.

The other kids and I pulled on our jeans and T-shirts and we hopped into the car.

'I couldn't sleep a wink,' she said to me, 'I was so excited about him coming home. Do you think …?' She did not finish what she wanted to say and the question she was too afraid to ask and the answer I would have been too afraid to give hung between us in the car.

She knew I didn't like her, knew I didn't approve of her, knew I didn't think she was good enough for my son. She was certainly beautiful and I was never openly rude to her but she must have seen disapproval in my eyes. She behaved in ways that I found intolerable. Sometimes my son used my car to go to university. When he had the use of the car, he would pick me up from work. Often she would be with him and I would find her sitting in the front seat of the car, as if the car belonged to her and she seemed so settled there, so sure that she had the right to sit there, that I would find myself getting into the back seat. She would ring my son in the middle of the night to tell him how depressed she was and to insist that he come to see her immediately. I would hear my car being driven out of the garage at all hours. I could forgive her for her constant despair about life but I could not forgive her for not being clever and I did not want my son to be bound to a girl who saw herself as the helpless victim of life's cruelties.

We did not talk much on the way to the airport or while we stood, four deep, trying to peer through the Customs doors as they opened to let out an endless dribble of jet-lagged, lug-gage-laden passengers.

My son had gone overseas with his best friend. The fact that his best friend was a girl was something we all speculated about. Would they return as friends? Would they return as lovers? I must confess I greatly approved of his best friend and hoped that youth, sexuality and proximity might have lead to a transfer of affections.

There were large numbers of family and friends gathered at the airport to welcome them home. I caught a glimpse, through the doors, of a purple shirt and a bearded face.

'There he is,' I cried.

A few minutes later they emerged. I watched my son as he pushed his trolley out through the doors and we all shouted and waved. He made his way towards us and I watched carefully to see what would happen.

She stood apart, in her black and white dress, with her carefully coiffured hair and her long, elegant fingernails – stood apart, waiting for him to rush into her arms. I watched her. I ached for her.

He hugged his family first and other friends crowded around him, slapping him on the back, welcoming him home. Then he saw her. 'Oh, hi,' he said, turning towards her and he went over to her and kissed her on the cheek.

My son's travelling companion had been greeted by her family and friends and, as she picked up her belongings to leave, he suddenly swept her into his arms and hugged her, lifting her high up into the air. 'As for you,' he said, laughing into her eyes, 'I never want to see you again.' And then we knew. We all knew. Except for the girl. Standing apart. In her black and white dress. Her eyes wide with longing.

She took his hand in hers as we walked back to the car. She sat close to him in the back seat and cuddled up to him. He allowed this to happen but he did not give her his attention. He chattered all the way home, giving us snippets of his three months' overseas sojourn.

When we arrived home, she went down to his room with him. I don't know what happened there but an hour or so later he came upstairs and said she was going home. He needed a sleep but she would come with us that night to a family outing at a Lebanese restaurant, to celebrate the homecoming. She caught a taxi home.

After she'd left he talked to us. He told us that the relationship had to end, that he had come to this realization even before he had gone overseas, that the distance had given him the determination and the strength to end it. And then he confirmed what we already suspected, that his best friend had become his lover. It had happened in Paris, during the last few weeks of their trip. It had only happened because they had been staying at a friend's flat and the sleeping accommodation was such that they'd had to share a single bed.

'I don't know how to tell her,' he said. 'I'm a coward when it comes to things like this.' We talked about it and we tried to give him courage and support and eventually he agreed that it would be unkind to delay. He would have to tell her that night, after we'd all been out to dinner.

We picked her up to go to the restaurant. I saw her gaze into my son's eyes when she got into the car, looking for love and approval. They walked ahead of us, from the parked car to the restaurant. We were watching them, her arm possessively twined about his waist.

'It's like watching a lamb going to the slaughter,' my youngest son said to me. And it was.

It was an uncomfortable meal. We watched her trying to please him. We watched her large doe eyes search and seek. 'Do you love me?' the eyes asked and we watched his eyes flicker, falter, dodge away. It was terrible to watch. Knowing her fate. Knowing what was going to happen to her later that evening.

We went home and the other children and I went straight to bed. We did not want to witness anything.

They went down to my son's room. I lay awake, listening, but I heard nothing. Although I did not like her, I could identify with her grief. A few hours later I heard the car leaving the garage. It was done. He was driving her home.

The following week, when I visited my enigmatic lover, I said to him: 'You're right. We do seek approval in each other's eyes. And if that's true of all people, then it must also be true of you. You do want me to approve of you, don't you?'

He gave me a perfectly predictable response: 'Now, then, how would you like a nice cup of tea?'

THE MAN WITH THE MAGIC PHALLUS

(Published in Moments of Desire – Penguin – 1989)

My husband and I have what is called an 'open marriage'. We're a modern, sophisticated couple. We're sure that it's possible to have a stable marriage and a little extra-marital fun without hurting anyone. The only rule we have is that our affairs are to be subordinate to our marriage.

I already have a lover, but our relationship is floundering. There's a new man I fancy. I met him quite by chance. I've agreed to go out to dinner with him, and my husband approves. He's going to mind the children while I go out and enjoy myself. That's only fair. After all, I babysit while he's out with his mistress.

I meet this new man and we go to a Chinese restaurant for dinner. He is, in many ways, every woman's dream. He is totally charming, disarming, self-confident. There is a twinkle in his eye and an assurance in his bearing that says he can have any woman he wants. I tell him that I have a husband and a lover. He says that doesn't bother him at all. He is in no hurry. He has infinite patience and time. He does not rush me, push me or make any sexual advances. He sits back, quite sure that I will come to him, waiting for me to make the first move. During dinner he tells me delightful and humorous stories of his early life in Hungary. He tells me of war experiences, smuggling, screwing in telephone booths. I feel that here is a man who has really lived a full and adventurous life. I've never been so genuinely delighted in a man's company. My somewhat gloomy husband and my despairing lover shrink beside this handsome man who makes me laugh and laugh.

He still makes no move. He goes on being totally, effortlessly charming. I am very easily won. As we leave the restaurant and go to cross the road, it is I who take his hand. He responds with a pressure of warmth, but still takes no advantage of me. We sit in his car. Now it's his turn to move. He kisses me and I am surprised by the warmth and passion of his kiss. I can sense that he is a good lover, and I tell him so. He, evidently, feels the same about me. But there's no hurry. We arrange a meeting during the day in a week's time.

I go home and my husband's awake, waiting for me, wanting to know what I've done. What was he like? Did I go to bed with him? I don't want to talk about it. I want to be left alone. He makes me tell him all about the evening. I have to go over every detail – the dinner, the kissing in the car, the plans for a further meeting. 'You're going to go to bed with him aren't you!' he says, his own excitement mounting. 'I know you are.'

'I'm not sure,' I reply, wanting to keep something to myself.

'Tell me again how he kissed you,' he demands, starting to make love to me. What he's asking me to do makes me shudder. He doesn't worry about foreplay but starts to thrust himself into me. 'Talk about it!' he says. 'Tell me what you feel when he kisses you.' I long to remain silent but I can't refuse him and I let the words he wants to hear tumble out of me. With a final, hammering charge he comes inside me, and then it's over and I'm glad it's over, and he lets me go, and I am, for the briefest moment, free.

The week seems long to me. I want this new man, and it feels good to be starting a new sexual adventure. When I get to his place and into his bed, I can see at once that I'm in the hands of an expert. He is cool, careful, perfect. He brings me to powerful orgasm with calm precision. Then he comes and, at that point, I am confronted with what I consider to be the eighth wonder of the world – his penis stays erect, and it is to remain that way for the next two hours.

Afterwards we talk. He tells me that I have a very rare sexual capacity and that, of the thousands of women he's made love to, only one other woman exhibited the strength of orgasm that I seem to be capable of. He proceeds to give me a careful, scientific analysis of our lovemaking, trying to teach me to be aware of my vagina and its potential. He intrigues me. I've never met a sex expert before. He has, he admits, devoted his entire life, from the time he turned eighteen to his present forty-four years, to making love to women. I am, of course, delighted and flattered to find that I have such a capable cunt. He is the master, I the willing pupil. He lures me into a world where sex dominates, where orgasm is the prize, where all that is valued is the quality of the coming – an orgiastic banquet, a physical feast, where art of the performance rather than emotion is the measure of success. No breathtaking passionate hunger with him, but rather the slow, deliberate excitation, the building climb to passion, the holding back, the going forward, the artistic weaving towards the unbelievable come.

He is a shift worker and I work odd hours. We can fit in many daytime meetings. I go to his place five days a week. This excessive extra-marital indulgence contravenes the agreement I've made with my husband, but I don't care.

What is it that he is doing for me? It is not that he is making love to me but that he gives me free rein, allows me to examine and explore and extend my own sexuality. He is always in control, simply there – the ever-erect penis on which I work my own way, in my own time, to my own end. His orgasm is immaterial to him and to me. He is just the vehicle of my self-discovery. I teach myself to attain the mysterious multiple orgasm. I stop only when my legs ache or my back aches – my cunt could go on forever. I am Woman – powerful, unleashed.

I give myself totally to this awakened sexuality without regard to possible consequences. I am hooked, trapped, the willing victim of an insatiable lust. I am my cunt. Nothing else is.

My husband is furious. I have castrated him, reduced him to powerless frustration. He cannot compete. I throw in his face the fact that some other man is able to make me respond in this extraordinary way. It is intolerable to him to find that I have a sexuality that he could never unlock, a sexual expression that he will never witness. He feels bitter, rejected, jealous.

My other lover, whose relationship with me has been primarily intellectual, feels equally hurt. How can I, he wants to know, prefer sexual, animal gratification to what he has to offer? I thumb my nose at the two of them. I'd throw them both away for the man with the magic prick.

I become, for a while, a kind of sexual football. I am thrown among the three of them, being screwed into a stupor. Sometimes I go to bed with all three of them on the same day. I do it deliberately – just to see if I can climax with each of them. If my husband thinks I've been with either of the others, he wants me all the more. 'I don't care,' he says, 'I don't care who you screw as long as you save some for me.' And I don't care about anything at all any more. From morning till night my only thought is for the sexuality that has somehow taken over my being.

And what is he, this man of the magic phallus with whom I wallow and stuff and gorge my insatiable sexual gluttony? He has been many things – professional gambler, smuggler, conman, thief. He entertains me constantly with stories of excitement and danger and I experience, through him, what it is to be an adventurer in an unstable and unpredictable world.

I am lying beside him. He is quiet at the moment. I am lying close to him, his arms around me. 'Have you ever killed anyone?' I ask, softly. I hear the 'Yes' from his heartbeat before I hear it from his lips.

Now I hear stories of a different kind – of murder and survival, of torture and imprisonment. He had been, he tells me, a smuggler with a difference. He had smuggled Jews out of communist Hungary and brought medicines and drugs back into the country. All this had been done for very high payment but within the boundaries of a strict, definitive moral code. He and his friend had been caught and imprisoned and his friend had been executed. He tells me now of torture, of having all his toe-nails pulled out and his teeth smashed. I understand now why his mouth is a glittering mass of gold fillings.

And then he tells me of revenge. Six guards, he says, inflicted torture upon him and, after his release from prison, he had sought out and killed five of them. The sixth had come to Australia and he, himself, came here originally, he tells me, to find and murder this man. I shiver beside him. Is he making this up? I don't think so. I sense his inner violence and I feel that he is telling me the truth.

And all this explains something else about him. His heart is ice. He never feels. He is a machine. 'Don't ever fall in love with me,' he warns. 'I'm not capable of loving.' Of course, I do not heed his warning.

We have a big party at our house and I invite my new lover. He buys me an expensive, black, hand-embroidered, Rumanian dress. My husband is furious, but I don't care, and I flaunt my lover's generosity. He buys himself a black, silk shirt for the occasion, and he looks so suave and handsome.

At the party my lover ignores me. He dances all night with a friend of mine who does not know that he and I are lovers. I watch him flirt with her. I tell myself that my lover can't spend all evening with me. If he did, everyone would know that we are lovers and, as I'm still married, I should keep my affair secret. But I notice that my husband has no such sense of propriety, and he's deliberately staying with his mistress. I am mortified and would like the floor to open and swallow me up.

I know that my lover is having an affair with my friend. I sense it. I ask him outright and he denies it, but I know he's lying. I want to ask her but I can't. One day I see her driving along in her car. She has a dreamy, wanton, sexual look on her face. I know she's going to him. An hour later I drive past his flat and I can see that her car is parked outside.

I see him that night. I am full of venom, anguish, complaint, hostility, criticism. His face is impassive, the cold veneer I can never penetrate. No feeling there. Had he ever, he wants to know, said he loved me? Had we ever agreed upon fidelity? He was my friend, my lover, always available when I needed him, his door always open, his cock always ready. What more did I expect?

'Love,' I want to cry, 'Love!'

THE LOGICAL MAN

I'm a rational, logical man. Always have been. I take pride in my ability to see clearly ahead, to anticipate the consequences of my actions, to see twenty steps in front of me. Logic. If you follow logic you can't go wrong. But this problem I'm facing right now is a bit difficult. I'm not sure how to solve it. Of course, it has to end. I can't live with her any longer. This grovelling, hysterical woman, begging for love. Thirteen years I've put up with her. Been a good husband, a good father, a good provider – everyone says so.

Yesterday I was sure of what I'd do, but today's a bit different. She's been away for ten days and she's come back looking all smooth and warm and brown. She's not wearing a bra and I can see her nipples through her T-shirt. She went away snivelling and broken and she's come back all self–contained and strong and I'm not sure any more. I want to touch those rubber tits of hers. But the kids are all over her. They've missed her – can't leave her alone. And her eyes are laughing at me because she sees how much I want her.

Bitch! Just look at her. So smug and sure of herself. You can tell she hasn't spent the last ten days in a state of celibacy. I wonder who the hell she's been to bed with?

Two weeks ago she was begging and pleading, saying she loved me, had always loved me, would always love me. She said she wanted to start again, to be faithful, to make our marriage work. And I said I'd think about it while she was away and decide whether I'd leave her or not.

I remember what it was like, that first night I met her. It was at a party. She was little and bright and gay. We talked and laughed and drank and everything was just right. We went off together in my car and we drove down to Ben Buckler, just overlooking Bondi Beach. We breathed on the windows and steamed them all up and we took off our clothes and hopped into the back seat and made love all night. I was a virgin. I'd have been faithful to her forever, I loved her so much.

She never understood me. Could I help it if I wanted her so much? I wanted to make love to her every time I touched her. I wanted her endlessly, day and night. I had to hold her all the time – while she was washing the dishes or hanging out the clothes or cooking the dinner. I couldn't leave her alone. Isn't that what loving a woman is all about? It's logical and reasonable, isn't it? If you love a woman then you want to make love to her all the time.

Neurotic she was, really neurotic. Said I was suffocating her. Said she needed a bit of space around herself. What the hell did she mean by 'space'? All I did was love her, love her all the time. Weird ideas she had about loving. Said I was all over her too much, wouldn't let her be herself. I think I was perfectly reasonable about the whole thing. Look what I did when this women's liberation business came in! Encouraged her, that's what I did. Let her go to work. Helped to look after the kids. Did the family washing every day – nappies, wet sheets and all. You can't say I didn't do my share.

Couldn't win with her. She really got strange. Didn't want to make love any more. Kept finding excuses or falling asleep. Said it was her way of holding onto herself. Rubbish! What was she on about? I know the kids got her down but I gave her as much help as I could. No matter what I did she went on rejecting me. Every time I made love to her it was like breaking through some barrier before I could get at her. I tell you, it was depressing.

So, anyway, we both started playing around a bit. Found herself a boyfriend, she did. Went off with him once a week. I didn't mind because I fancied this girl at the office. Nice enough girl she was. So I started up with her. Never rejected me – I always turned her on. Everything was good fun, in the beginning. Laughed about it, the wife and I. Did we ever laugh. Thought we were very clever. Marriage gets a little shaky – liven it up with a bit of extra-marital dalliance. Makes the marriage stronger. So it did, for a while.

Then suddenly the whole world falls apart. My wife meets this guy. I can tell he's a conman from the first time I set eyes on him but she's taken in. He only wants her body but she doesn't see that. She thinks he loves her and loses all control. She starts going to his place five and six times a week and she doesn't want me at all, not at all any more. And I feel this terrible emptiness and despair because I know she's the sexiest woman in the world and she's giving it all to him and none to me and I want to cry I love her so much and I'm so empty without her. And so I go more and more to this other girl and I start to love her because I'm that sort of man. I need to love a woman, to feel loved and warm and secure. So our marriage goes on. We live in the same house but there's nothing left of our relationship and we hold on because we've got children and the whole thing is such a damned mess we don't know what to do about it.

And then this conman does just what I've been expecting him to do. He leaves my wife and takes up with some other woman. And she comes crying back to me, begging and plead-ing, asking me to forgive her, wanting to give our marriage another go.

THE BOOK OF LIFE

And now I get my own back on her. Well, she deserves it, doesn't she? Our roles are reversed for a change. She keeps wanting me to make love to her and I keep refusing her to make up for all those times when she rejected me.

It's not just a matter of revenge. It's more complicated than that. I've come to love this other girl, haven't I? And she loves me. I can't just turn off her and onto my wife, now can I? That's not reasonable. I know I've got to make up my mind between the two of them so I tell my wife to go away for a holiday for ten days and I'll stay home and look after the kids and decide what to do.

And while she's away it's so peaceful. I realize I've come to hate her. I can't stand her hysterics. I don't love her any more. I'm sick of her neurotic ways. All I want is for this marriage to come to an end.

But now, today, I'm not so sure. As I said, she's come back so brown and sexy and her eyes look at me with wanting and with love. I watch her as she smiles and laughs with her kids and every time I look at her I want her and I keep going up and touching her and hugging her and I don't seem to be my calm and logical self. I don't really know what I'm going to do.

It's a long, hot day. I keep wanting her and she keeps wanting me and we both know that we have to wait until the kids have gone to bed.

Somehow the day goes by and as soon as the kids are asleep I grab her and rush her to our bed and we can hardly wait to get our clothes off and we tear at each other as if we've never made love before. When it's over I push her away and I look into her eyes.

'Now I'll tell you what I've decided to do,' I say, feeling calm and reasonable once again. 'I'm going to leave you.'

And I watch her eyes stare at me, wounded and vacant. She turns her head away. I can see the tears trickling sideways down her cheek and falling into her hair. I'm a rational, logical man.

THE TELEPHONE MAN

(Published in The Short Story – Inprint Vol.8 No.1 – 1985)

This is the story of Bill, the telephone man. He's not really a telephone man at all. It's just that the kids and I met him one hot summer day outside a public telephone box. Ever since then we've affectionately referred to him as "the telephone man".

We were going to the beach and I had no change to pay the toll on the Harbour Bridge so I'd stopped at a shop. I'd bought the kids some chewing gum. Of course, they didn't need any chewing gum. It's just that I needed the change. Under the promise of severe punishment (perhaps I'd even threatened murder) I'd made them stay in the car while I made my purchase. If they all tumbled out now I'd never get to the beach.

I felt great that day – in my sexy beach dress with my deep suntan. As I started to walk back to the car this man called out, 'You've got you hands full there!'

'I sure have,' I smiled.

'Where are you going with all those kids?' he asked.

I started to get back into the car. 'To the beach, of course. It's such a beautiful day.'

'How can you manage so many kids all by yourself?' he wanted to know.

'When they are your own children, you just have to,' I replied, smiling.

I looked at him. Early thirties. Khaki work shorts. Work boots. Well built. Pleasant face. Straight, light brown hair. Small, neat moustache.

'Why don't you come with us?' I asked, knowing he wouldn't come, but feeling that I wouldn't mind if he did.

'I haven't got a costume with me,' he said.

'That's OK. We're going to a nudist beach,' I retorted, hoping to shock him.

'Are you really?' He came to my side of the car and leaned down to talk to me through the window. 'I'd love to come, but I have to work today. Can I come with you another day?'

I liked him and I felt great. 'Why not?' I replied.

'Look,' he said. 'Are you free?'

I laughed with genuine delight. The extraordinary incongruity of the scene hit me. Here was I, a lady with a carload of kids, being asked if I was "free". But freedom, I suppose, is a matter of the spirit and certainly, in every real sense of the word, I felt "free". I started to like him more and more. The circumstances of our meeting were so strange that I began to read into the whole situation, the incomprehensible hand of fate.

The kids were becoming restless, bored and quite obnoxious. They wanted to get to the beach. He ignored them.

'I'm building this house,' he said. 'I'm moving into it quite soon. When I do, I'll ring you up and invite you over.'

'I'd like that,' I said. I gave him my name and phone number.

I didn't hear from the telephone man. I was really disappointed. There had been such an immediate and spontaneous attraction between us that I was sure he'd ring me the next day. Every time we passed that telephone box (and I often drove past it on purpose) I'd say to the kids, 'Have a look will you. See if you can see the telephone man.' It became quite a game. But then, my children love such games. And they love to give titles to boyfriends I might have – like "the man from the beach" or "the man with the motorbike" or "the man with the funny accent". I dreamed many dreams of the telephone man, but the telephone man never called.

Six months later he contacted me. 'It's Bill,' he said. 'I bet you don't even remember me.'

'I do! I do!' I cried excitedly. Divorced ladies have a terrible habit of seeing any new man as the answer to all their prayers. 'Why did you take so long to ring me?'

'I couldn't invite you over until I'd finished at least one room in my house,' he answered.

I'm ashamed to say that I made a terrible mess of my five-month relationship with Bill. I wanted more than he could give. He offered friendship and I wanted love. The failure of our relationship is, however, not the point of this story. What I wanted to tell you about is that Bill is no ordinary man and his house is no ordinary house.

When Bill was fifteen he decided that he was going to build himself a house. From that day on he has gone ahead, step by step, purposefully pursuing and fulfilling his dream. Most people set themselves impossible goals. He set himself an achievable fantasy and it is this that distinguishes him from most people I know. His dream was to build the house all by himself. For this purpose he learned every trade necessary for the building of his house. He is builder, carpenter, bricklayer, painter, plumber, electrician.

He likes to build his house a little at a time. No room is really finished. The whole house has an air of a work in progress. It also has the feeling of a work of art. It is full of marvellous incongruities. The lounge-room has beautiful chandeliers and uncovered drainpipes. In the corner there are highly polished wooden shelves displaying tasteful and delicate shells and orna-ments. Two feet away lies an open tool box, a jar of dirty paint brushes and the grill of an old Holden car. A small, gilt-edged mirror hangs on a temporary wall of corrugated iron. In the bathroom he has an exquisite double sink of marble, topped by unfinished brickwork. Out of this brickwork, a piece of wire protrudes on which he hangs his towel. The kitchen has a magnificent, enormous electric stove and oven. He has had this amazing piece of equipment for quite some time but he hasn't bothered to have it connected to the electricity supply. He cooks for himself on a small, old, single-element griller.

'What will you do,' I asked, 'when you've finished your house?'

'I'll build a big swimming pool out in the backyard,' he replies, 'and I won't be using any bull-dozers. I'll dig it out myself – shovel by shovel.' And he will. I know it.

Sometimes I go and visit him. I went there the other day. I went because I was sad and because, somehow, both Bill and his house exude a calm strength in which I can breathe and rest and feel secure.

He gave me what I came for but when I left his house I felt, somewhat strangely, that I was taking a feeling of sadness with me. As I looked at the big house behind me I knew that I had left my own sorrow behind but I had taken his sorrow away with me.

What would happen to him, I wondered, when he had finished his house? What would he do with his four bedrooms and his two bathrooms and his big swimming pool? The house is his dream and his alone. No one can ever share it. No woman will ever cook in his magnificent kitchen. No child's laughter will ever be heard in his empty rooms. Day by day, week by week, year by year, with single-minded devotion and with loving care he builds this great monument to his own skills. Brick by brick constructs the walls of his own tomb.

I hurried home to be met by a flurry of child warmth, soft flesh, exuberant voices, sticky caresses and I felt grateful for the whirling life about me.

HE AND SHE – AN ADULT FAIRY TALE

He met her at the nudist beach. He watched her ample arse move up and down as she made her frequent trips to cool off in the sea. He wanted to feel that arse resting warm in the curve of his stomach, his bollocks, his thighs – so he followed her into the sea.

'Can you float?' he asked.

She looked at him. An amiable, friendly young man. Much better approach than the usual, 'Do you come here often?'

'Yes,' she replied.

'Will you show me how?' he asked.

'Why not,' she replied.

She tried to show him how to float but he was hopeless. They laughed a lot and went back up to sit on the sand.

He had left his wife three weeks ago and hadn't had a screw since then. He was determined to have this one. She didn't know that.

She liked him because when he ascertained that she had been separated from her husband for a year, he immediately asked how her children coped with such a situation. This surprised her. Men usually didn't give a damn about her children. They just wanted to establish her availability.

Because she liked him and because she was lonely and because he was a stranger to her city, she asked him to come to dinner the following night. The children were away for a week with their father so she had the house to herself. Because he liked her and because he still longed to feel that beautiful arse, he accepted.

She promised to come back to the beach the next day but he didn't think she would come. He slept the night on the beach because he really had nowhere else to go and from the time the sun rose in the morning he paced up and down the beach, longing for her to come. She came and when she saw him like that, pacing impatiently, so anxious for her to come, she allowed herself to respond with a rush of joy.

They talked for a while, but obviously neither could wait to get down to the business of exploring each other's bodies. As they were leaving the beach he whispered to her, 'I think I should warn you. My cock always stays hard.' She felt her cunt contract. In what seemed like an endless stream of lovers, she'd only ever known one cock like that. A long time ago. If there was anything in the world that she could do with right now it was a man with a cock that stayed hard.

They entered then, for six weeks, that wondrous state of loving that most people experience once in a lifetime and feel that no one has ever experienced before – the rapture when passion serves only to kindle passion, when bodies are one, locked in mutual hunger.

He knew it was love. Despite the hundreds of women and two wives, he had never believed in a thing called 'love'. Now he knew what the stories and songs were all about.

She thought it was love because she wanted so badly to be in love. Because her body was so totally fused with his, she mistook fusion for love.

After six weeks she wanted to become a person again. He couldn't understand that. He wanted to be love's slave forever.

She tried to explain herself, to define her needs, her intellect, her sense of self. He did not want to understand.

An impasse. The He – She split. The heavy scenes. Ending always in the only possible way – a passionate, tumbling return to oneness.

She had a magic cunt and he had a magic cock and together they created unheard of music. Sometimes, at the touch of his tongue, her juices fountained into the air and flooded the bed.

'I've fucked my way around the world three times,' he'd say, 'and I've never come across a cunt like this.' She wasn't sure if she liked having a cunt like this. It frightened her to be lost in his sexual world.

'The pity of it is,' he'd say, 'no one will ever believe me.' He would have liked to exhibit her, like a freak at a sideshow.

He persisted in believing that all love must be good. He thought her beautiful; he worshipped her; he wanted to give her his love and adoration twenty-four hours a day, seven days a week, forever. How could that be bad? She tried to explain that she couldn't breathe.

She liked to be with him. He was romantic and sentimental, loving and gay, a delightful child. But by the end of the day she wanted to scream.

He would say, 'I cannot imagine life without you.' Every time he said that her heart would sink, for she could not envisage going on much longer.

He could not cope with a part-time relationship. All he lived for were the hours he spent with her. She could not cope with a full-time relationship. She had her job as a teacher. She had her children. She started to long for the hours she could spend alone. He was unhappy and she was unhappy but no matter how unhappy they made each other there was always that oneness to return to, to enjoy, to exalt in, to get lost in, to wonder at.

Finally she got so unhappy that he had to admit defeat. If he really loved her, he would have to let her go. So he found the strength to end it. She cried. He couldn't understand why she was crying; after all, she was the one who wanted it to be over. 'I have so much to give you,' he said, 'and you want so little of it, and when I take that little away all you can do is cry.' She went on crying. She couldn't stop. 'I feel as if my legs and arms have been chopped off,' he said. 'I have nothing left to live for.' She went on crying. It seemed that her tears would never cease.

So He and She parted. And there was, for both of them, a time of terrible sadness because, within the awful mess of their relationship, there had always been that flaming core of oneness that neither of them had ever known before.

TWO LEOS

Where is she, my darling, precious little girl? She's sent me a letter telling me that it's all over, that I'm too old, too old. Behind the house grey clouds hang over the mountain and drops of rain fall down my cheeks.

Too old! If only she'd known me thirty years ago. Two stone lighter and a permanent erection. A wicked, cruel thing. To find her now. So late in life. Too old.

My precious darling, lying on my tummy, her legs drawn up frog-like on her log, her big-bellied old lion lying beneath her. She would take me with her hand and rub me against her moist rose-bud, back and forth across her little mound, placing me exactly where she wanted me to be and that is all I ever asked … to be her servant, to be her slave, to be the object of her satisfaction. Moving me back and forth, her mouth locked on mine, tongues seeking, hearts beating, moving me back and forth, plunging me into her warmth, holding me safe inside her, guiding me so that I could touch exactly the right place, in exactly the right way. Coming closer, closer. Exploding over me, shouting in the folds of my shoulder, flooding me.

Dearest darling, precious girl. Lying beside me in the curve of my arm. I turn and our tummies touch. Both born in August though many years apart. Two Leos. Two lions. Breathing with the same rhythm. Heartbeats synchronized. Flaming with the same fire. Gently breathing each other's breath. Our skins touch top to toe. Through the pores of our skin we breathe each other's essence. In. Out. In. Out. Pure osmosis. She touches my nipple, gently, caressing, rubbing and I touch hers and feel it rise, stiffening beneath my soft fingertips. I clip my nails and file them smooth so there's no chance of hurting her. I stroke her hair and she strokes mine and I press my mouth more firmly against hers; twin tongues touch, devour and consume.

Her hand moves across to brush my nipple again, back and forth with her open palm, then rolling it lightly in her fingertips. Her tummy presses urgently into mine and between her legs I feel my manhood come to life, throbbing gently against her thigh. We cling, suffused by the self-same glow, one body, one circle, one life. She makes little sounds in her throat and so do I – murmurs of pleasure, purring of cats. Lions coupling.

We move apart and I stretch across and help myself to some magic cream. I rub the soothing coolness onto her clitoris and she rubs silky cream onto my penis. We lie on our sides. She takes my penis into both her hands, stroking, caressing, teasing, rubbing beneath the rim of his head and causing him to weep pearls of joy onto her fingertips. I have one arm around her, holding her tight, and the other inside her, my thumb caressing her rising rose-bud. Let the moment last forever and ever. Let me die like that, suspended in ecstasy.

Our bodies yearn for union and press closer and closer to each other. My penis is almost touching her and she guides it between her thighs, letting it touch her clitoris, moving herself across it, not allowing it to enter her, teasing me, rubbing herself harder and harder against me until I think I'll go mad, explode too soon, spoil it all. She is relentless and determined. She moves with swifter and swifter passion towards her own conclusion. When the moment is right she grants me entry and I plunge into her, my old heart pounding, chest aching, panting, pumping my seed into the altar of her being. I clutch her close to me and kiss her sweet mouth, tasting on her breath the scent of my own semen.

I stroke her. I caress her. I cannot bear to let her go. Precious moment of after-loving. Dear little girl. I would like to hold her in my arms forever.

Too old, she says. I am a symbol of death, she says. It is like incest, she says. She doesn't want to hurt me, she says, but she has to go — flee, flee before it's too late. Flee from the father, flee from death.

What rubbish! What nonsense! Too old for her? And yet I know, I know that I will die, that I will leave her loveless, that her need for love is so boundless, so fathomless, so consuming that she fears the darkness, the emptiness, the space of loved ones lost.

I move through my hollow house, old man, old lion, wandering in the desert, licking his wounds, longing for her sweet caress, the soft, gentle touch that kindles an old man's fire.

I take up my pen and I write to her, my darling, my precious one. I pour myself onto the paper. I flood her with golden words of love. Drink me, darling girl, drink me. Take the incestuous cup. Hold it in your hands. Drink deep. Slake your thirst on me for just a little longer.

ADEL THE ANIMATOR

At Hurgarda, by the Red Sea, I met Adel the Animator. I thought an animator drew cartoon figures for films but, in Egypt, the word has quite a different meaning. An animator brings people to life and so, in Egyptian tourist hotels, along the Red Sea, animators are employed to bring joy and delight into the lives of the tourists staying at their hotel. An animator's job is to keep the guests happy. He is on call twenty-four hours a day. If the guests want to see the sun rising across the Red Sea, the animator must get up at 4.30 am, wake the interested people and organize them into watching this splendid phenomenon. If the guests want to snorkel on a coral reef, it is the animator's duty to organize the expedition. If the guests want to do nothing but laze around in deckchairs, sunbaking or reading books, then the animator will emerge from his room with a soccer ball and excitedly kick it around by himself in the hope that some of the guests will join him in his obligatory effort to involve them in fun, fun, fun.

When I arrived in Hurgarda, by the Red Sea, the last thing I wanted was to be taken over by the animators. However, my friend and I found ourselves in Hurgarda in late December. It was not the tourist season. The bitter wind, grey skies and heavy seas made the prospect of snorkelling unattractive and the sparsity of guests meant it was inevitable that we would be singled out by the animators for attention. The idea of two women, dining alone, must have seemed appallingly inappropriate to any male Egyptian, let alone to a hotel animator whose job, after all, was to eliminate such an unseemly sight.

So it was that I met Adel, one of the two animators employed by our hotel. I felt sorry for him when he sat down to join us with his ever-ready smile. I wanted to tell him that we did not need to be entertained, that we were quite capable of entertaining each other. Such a declaration of self-sufficiency would not have been believed so we welcomed Adel the Animator with cautious smiles of our own and very soon we felt quite comfortable in his company. He ordered our meal with brisk authority and our first reward for having him at our table was to be served swiftly with appetizing food – something we had learned one could not always rely upon in Egypt.

We talked of his job and he, of course, professed to find every moment of it rewarding and satisfying. He came from a middle-class, educated, Cairo family and I was not surprised to learn that, in Egypt, a university degree is a requirement for an animator. He wanted us to understand that he was not like other Egyptians. He felt himself to be like a foreigner in Cairo, fearful of crowds, intolerant of dust and quite incapable of bargaining in the bazaar. Who had ever heard of an Egyptian who could not bargain? No, he did not belong in Egypt and if he could not travel as much as he wished to, then his only salvation lay in the relative peace and calm and purity of Hurgarda, by the Red Sea.

And so it was that he told me a story of his journey to Yugoslavia by way of illustrating to me how modern and westernized he was in his attitudes, how far and distanced he was from the primitive values and beliefs of traditional Egyptian Islam.

And because I'm always hungry for stories, I sat there in the almost empty, circular restaurant, with its panoramic, full-length glass doors; its modern, stained-glass skylights; its garish, coloured, patterned mirrors – I sat there and listened to Adel the Animator and I heard his strange tale of East and West, of repression and desire, of lust and love.

Adel had been excited as he boarded the plane for Belgrade. He knew nothing about Yugoslavia but he was eager to experience a new country. He had three months free from university studies and he intended to spend a few weeks in Yugoslavia and then go on to Greece. Just before the plane landed Adel asked the people around him whether any of them knew of a good cheap hotel in Belgrade and a fellow traveller gave him the name of a hotel near the university.

The taxi-driver, however, misunderstood Adel and took him to the university itself. Adel found a few students who spoke English and they directed him to the University Youth Hostel.

Adel presented his passport to the person on the desk and was met with a strange response.

'You're Egyptian, aren't you? Would you like a drink?'

'Yes, thank you, I would,' Adel replied.

The desk clerk went away to get Adel a drink and another clerk arrived at the desk, glanced at the passport and then smiled at Adel and said, 'I see you're Egyptian. Would you like a drink?' Before Adel could reply, this second clerk dashed away, calling over his shoulder, 'I'll just get the manager.'

The manager of the hostel arrived moments later, looked at Adel's passport and said, 'So, you're Egyptian. Would you like a drink?' Adel, by this time, was feeling worried and confused. Why was everyone treating him so nicely? Why were they all offering him drinks? Then the manager explained that they needed Adel's help. A young Egyptian man had arrived at the hostel a week ago. They could tell that he was in some kind of trouble but as he spoke no English and they spoke no Arabic they had been unable to communicate with him. They wanted Adel to speak to this fellow-Egyptian and to find out what was wrong and how he could be helped. The thrice offered drink arrived and Adel was encouraged to sit down and enjoy it, having agreed to help the manager in the matter of the non-English speaking Egyptian.

And so it happened that Adel met Abrahim. Abrahim had the kind of face that made everyone laugh whenever he spoke. Adel assured me that it was not what he said that made you laugh but the way he spoke, the way he moved the features of his face. Even when what he was saying was sad or serious, you could not help yourself. You had to laugh and laugh. Abrahim was a mechanic and I must say that Adel spoke the word 'mechanic' in such a way as to indicate that a person so labelled was the very lowest form of humanity. Indeed, if I think very carefully, I do believe that the word Adel used was not 'mechanic' but 'mechanical'. Yes, that was it. With a tone of definite disdain, Adel said to me, 'Abrahim was a mechanical.'

Abrahim had been brought to Yugoslavia with a group of Egyptian 'mechanicals' to learn how to service machines made in Yugoslavia but he had lost the rest of the group. He had become separated from them at the airport and had no idea where they were. He could understand no one. No one could understand him. Somehow he had found himself at the youth hostel and they had taken him in. He had not known what to do so each day he had gone out and wandered the streets and looked and looked into the faces of people walking by. What he was looking for was someone with dark hair and dark skin. He thought that if he could find someone with dark hair and dark skin then perhaps that person would be able to speak Arabic. If he found a person with dark hair and dark skin who could speak Arabic then he could ask that person what he should do. But he did not find any person with dark hair and dark skin. He found only people with fair hair and fair skin. The hostel manager had written down the name and address of the hostel for him so, at the end of each day's searching, he would show the card to people until, somehow, he would manage to get back to the hostel. He was so happy to see Adel, to talk to Adel, to be understood by Adel.

Adel offered to help Abrahim find the other members of his group but Abrahim did not think that was a good idea. Abrahim thought he was in Europe. Abrahim thought that he was free. He thought that there was a whole exciting world right here for him to enjoy and he wanted to explore that world now that he had found someone who could understand him.

What Abrahim wanted was a woman. What Abrahim wanted was sex. Abrahim was consumed by lust and desire.

Did I understand, Adel wanted to know, what it must be like for a boy like Abrahim? Brought up in the narrow, traditional, Egyptian ways of Islam? Did I realize that boys and girls were not even allowed to play with each other after the age of seven? Did I know that older boys and girls were allowed no social contact whatsoever? Did I understand what it was like for an Arabic boy to live in a world of veiled women, never to have known the sight of a woman's face, the touch of a woman's hand? Abrahim, at the age of twenty-three, was driven mad by a desire for sexual experience. That was why he had left Egypt. That was why he had come to Yugoslavia. He had to know what it was like to have a woman.

No, Abrahim definitely did not think it was a good idea to find the other 'mechanicals'. He thought he should stay at the hostel with Adel and put the pain and anguish of the previous week behind him. What Abrahim wanted was to have a good time.

That day Adel and Abrahim moved into a different room at the youth hostel. Five people were to occupy this room – an Australian man, the two Egyptians and two girls from Denmark.

Abrahim kept asking Adel was it really true? Were girls actually going to sleep in the same room as men? Adel tried to explain that such a thing was quite natural for Europeans and quite common at youth hostels but Abrahim could not believe it.

Adel went out to buy cigarettes and, when he returned, Abrahim had disappeared. Two hours later Adel found him in the communal bathroom, cleaning his teeth. In this bathroom there was a shower and next to the shower was a small, coin-operated machine for washing and drying underclothes. Abrahim had come into the bathroom to clean his teeth and, while he was doing so, one of the Danish girls had entered, stripped off her clothes, placed her underclothes into the little machine and stepped in to have a shower while her underclothes washed and dried. Abrahim was so amazed that he had stayed there in the bathroom cleaning his teeth, for two hours! He wanted to observe all the comings and goings. No, Abrahim was not going to miss a thing. That night Abrahim could hardly eat anything at all. His mouth was so raw and sore from excessive teeth-cleaning.

The five in the room became firm friends. They ate together, went sight-seeing together, laughed together. The Australian man, the two Danish girls, Anna and Helga, and Adel spoke in English. Abrahim could not communicate with anyone except Adel but that did not stop him enjoying himself. Abrahim spoke in Arabic and, even if the others did not understand him, they laughed and laughed whenever he spoke because, as Adel kept reminding me, that was the effect Abraham had on people. When Abrahim spoke, everyone laughed.

Abrahim wanted Adel to ask one of the Danish girls to sleep with him. Adel tried to explain that it did not work that way. There had to be a particular feeling between a man and a woman. If that particular feeling were there, then the man and the woman would, quite naturally, want to make love but if that particular feeling were not there, then such a thing was impossible. Abrahim wanted to know how to go about getting that particular feeling but Adel said that was something he could not explain in words. That was something that Adel could not teach him. It was something Abrahim would have to find out for himself. And, Adel added, it would be very difficult, indeed, probably impossible, for Abrahim to get anywhere with the Danish girls because they had no language in common and therefore Abrahim could not win them with words.

Nevertheless, Adel felt some sympathy for Abrahim's plight and he suggested getting rid of the Australian for the day and going for a picnic in the forest near the hostel. He told Abrahim that he, Adel, would go off with Anna and that would leave Abrahim and Helga alone.

Abrahim said, 'What do I have to do when we are alone?'

And Adel answered, 'I don't know what you have to do. It's up to you to find out. If it happens, it happens.'

Adel delayed Anna and they talked together while Abrahim disappeared into the forest with Helga. Adel, after a time, suggested to Anna that they should go back to the hostel. As the hours passed, Adel began to feel uncomfortable. He should not have helped Abrahim. He was sure that, in his madness to know a woman, Abrahim might well have raped Helga and he felt guilty for the part he had played.

When Abrahim and Helga returned to the youth hostel, five hours later, Adel knew that everything was alright. Abrahim had his arm about the girl and he called excitedly, 'Adel! Adel!' and he held up four fingers to show Adel how many times he had made love to Helga.

Helga was studying Medicine in Denmark but she said she would give it up for Abrahim. When the time came for Adel to leave Yugoslavia, Anna and the Australian man both decided to accompany him to Greece. But Helga would not leave her Abrahim. Abrahim thought that he should honour his work obligation in Yugoslavia. When his training was over, Helga would go back to Egypt with him and live with him there. She told Adel that she had always dreamed of loving such a man – a primitive man, a natural man – and she would never leave him. She would follow him forever.

Adel told her she was mad. He told her she could not give up her life in Denmark, her studies, her civilized future for the sake of a mere 'mechanical'. But she would not listen. She would not listen to Adel. She would not listen to Anna. All her life she had longed for a man like Abrahim. She had found him. She would never let him go.

It was obvious that, despite winning the love of a sophisticated Danish girl, Abrahim had not risen in Adel's estimation. Abrahim was still seen as an ordinary and inferior Egyptian and Adel's purpose in telling me this story was to establish his own superiority over the lowly Abrahim. He wondered, with wry bewilderment, how the cultivated Helga could have been satisfied with such a man.

'You're very quiet,' he said. 'Have you been listening? What do you think of my story?'

It was true that I had retreated, withdrawn myself from Hurgarda and from Adel because his story had touched upon my own past. Once I, too, had loved a primitive man, loved him with such exquisite passion that I thought I would be able to abandon the patterns of my life and follow him into an alien land. I did not follow him but as I sat listening to Adel the Animator, in Hurgarda, by the Red Sea, I felt gratified to know that some other woman, at some other time, in some other place, had found the courage to sacrifice everything for the love of a natural man.

THE FACE IN THE PHOTOGRAPH

I saw her again today. At the shopping centre. Riding up the escalator. I didn't want to take any notice of her. Madness frightens me. I saw her but I didn't want to see her so I turned my head away.

I made myself think of Christmas and the weekend away with the kids and all the food I had to buy and the last minute shopping that had to be done. I rushed here and there; a trolley of greengroceries, fresh bread rolls, chicken pieces, minced meat, ham and cheese.

I pushed my trolley onto the escalator and there she was again. This time she was travelling down the escalator and I was travelling up. I couldn't avoid looking at her. She was in my direct line of vision.

Dumpy, fiftyish, straggly short grey hair, lips moving incessantly. She held a photograph right up against her wild, red eyes. She held it so close to her eyes that she could not possibly have focused on it. But she knew the photograph. Knew the face. Knew it intimately. She talked all the time to the face in the photograph.

She came closer to me and I came closer to her. I watched her all the time but she did not see me watching her. Her eyes were rivetted on the face in the photograph. Her eyes leaked tears. Her left hand held the photograph tightly in place and her right hand mopped up the tears with a handkerchief. I came level with her and I could not take my eyes away from her face. Her eyes were so rheumy, so wet, so red – she must have spent all day watching the photograph, weeping the tears, wiping them up.

I turned my head as she passed me on the escalator. I wanted to see the photograph. It was the face of a young man in his twenties; pleasant looking, with straight dark hair and brown eyes. I wondered who he was. It was a modern photograph; the young man wore modern clothes. It must have been her son. I felt quite sure that it was her son who had driven her mad. How did he do it? Did he rob, rape, murder, take drugs, die a tragic death?

I have watched madness. My cousin went mad. When she was eighteen, her first boyfriend dropped her and she went to bed and stayed there for a year. When she got up she was no longer the same girl. She spent her life swinging between manic ecstasy and dark despair. Everyone said she went mad because she was jilted by her boyfriend but I don't know if that's true. I remember walking with her once along a country road. She was thirteen years old and I was twelve. 'I'm going to die when I'm forty,' she said to me. 'If I'm not dead by the time I reach forty, I'm going to kill myself.' And that's what happened. She died in a psychiatric hospital just after her fortieth birthday. They said it was heart failure but how is one to know.

I knew a boy who went mad. He was my children's baby sitter. He was gentle and soft and quiet but something drove him inwards. Something robbed him of reality. He dwelt in darkness. He wrote me strange, disjointed letters. The letters came day after day. His words made no sense but I understood that he was asking for my help. If I had known where he was I would have answered his plea but his letters gave no clue to his whereabouts. They were just like messages from outer space. The letters stopped one day. Just like that.

I had a lover once who was mad. It was love that drove him mad. I was the victim of his obsession. He wanted to be with me every minute of the day. He used to wake me up in the middle of the night, demanding to know the content of my dreams. I wanted to leave him after six weeks but it took four years to get rid of him. He used to tell me that if I tried to leave him he would kill me and put me in the attic. He would lay me on a bed of black velvet and dress me in Indian clothes and drape me with jewellery. He would spread out my hair and burn incense sticks around me. Then no one could have me. No one but himself. I know what madness is.

And I have felt madness, here, within the confines of my mind. I have heard it rumble and roar and rush through the tunnels of my brain, clamouring for the light. What would it take to set it free?

I have known anguish and despair, betrayal and pain. I have known loss and death and an emptiness so wide and deep that I thought I would never be able to crawl out of that chasm. But I've never ridden up and down the escalators, clutching at a face in a photograph.

COPACABANA

There's nothing wrong with Copacabana, except it's name. The Aborigines called the beach Tudibaring which seems to me to be an attractive and musical name. I suppose the developers of the area thought Copacabana a suitable and exotic name for this Central Coast resort. The streets have names like Del Rio, Fiesta, Del Mar, Vista.

I have a house there. Nestled on the side of the hill, facing east. I cannot see the waves breaking on the sand but I have a wide view of the ocean and, through the expansive sliding glass doors of my living room, I can see the houses on the hill of the opposite side of the valley and I can see the waves breaking on the rocks at the very end of Copacabana beach.

My house is like a ship, sailing on the ocean; not just because I can gaze at the wide horizon but because everything in the house is ship-shape. Everything has its place. Everything is neat. Everything harmonizes. The colours are cream and beige and brown. Even the plates and cooking utensils, the sheets and towels.

Colourful lorikeets strut up and down my verandah rail and giant white cockatoos live in the large tree next door. The cicadas are so numerous that their song suffuses the evening light. In the quiet of the night I can hear the waves breaking on the beach.

The house is my retreat from mess and motherhood. It is the place where I go to do my writing. My retreats are usually of short duration because I'm afraid of what will happen at the other place in my absence. This time my escape has lasted almost three weeks and I have begun to realize that mother-hood might well be over. They've had a plague of fleas down there, while I've been away. I thought I ought to go back to help out but the children told me not to. They said I should stay, up here, at Copacabana. The only way they managed to get rid of the fleas was by a total tidy-up and spring-clean of the house. When I go back, I will witness a miracle.

I have a pattern to my days, here at Copacabana. At 6 am I run 3.4 kilometres. I know the distance exactly because I measured it on the speedometer of the car. Then I have a shower and breakfast and read for half an hour or so. At 8 am I walk down to the beach-front and buy the newspaper, go down onto the sand, apply my block-out sun lotion and begin trekking up and down the beach. I walk to the Copacabana end first, then turn and walk right to the McMasters beach end, then back. I usually do this twice. I need to do all this before I feel ready to start on my writing.

While I walk, I think. It is not an active thinking but a rambling mode of thought, allowing scenarios of the past or the future to play themselves out as I march along the sand. I think of my children, their problems, their ambitions. I imagine their successes and my joy in their achievements. I think about making love. I think about writing books. I look at life, assess it, come to conclusions, make decisions.

While I walk, I also watch. I watch the contours of the headlands at each end of the beach. I watch the changing moods of the sea. This morning a sea mist clung to the beach and hung in the hollow formed where a rocky outcrop marks the beginning of Mc Masters beach. The sea was angry and vicious and, although I walked well up from the tide-line, occasional freakish waves lashed about my thighs.

I note the difference between the people at each end of the beach. The Copacabana end is very Australian. I am told that the Friday night barbecues at the Life-Saving club are dominated by men wearing their shorts and downing their cans of beer. I imagine that a similar function at McMasters beach would reveal a proliferation of elderly blue-rinsed matrons in their smart silks, sipping sherry.

I have no wish to socialize with anyone. I watch the families frolicking on the sea-edge. Mummies, daddies, little children – building sandcastles and constructing catchments to trap the ebbing ocean. As I walk along and watch them my only feeling is one of gratitude. I am so glad that these little children are not mine, so relieved that my years of that kind of parenting are over.

There are many kinds of dogs on the beach. Their owners walk along the sea-shore, throwing sticks or tennis balls into the sea for their dogs to retrieve. I like to watch them but I wouldn't want to own any of them. The beach abounds in boys with surfboards, wet-suits and patterns of coloured zinc cream decorating their faces. They look like members of an African tribe.

The other day I was walking towards the McMasters end of the beach when I saw a couple making their way slowly down to the water. I thought they were lovers, playing around. They were both facing the sea and they were hard against each other and they walked with the same steps, like tin soldiers with stiff legs, keeping time. The person behind was taller and held the other person tightly under the arms so that their bodies moved in perfect unison. I smiled to myself, amused by their antics, not paying them too much attention.

As I drew nearer I realized that this was no loving couple playing games. A mother, with her arms about her child, was guiding her totally spastic, adolescent daughter, step by pain-staking step, towards the sea. I did not want to embarrass them by staring so I looked away and continued walking but not before I saw the strain in the woman's face, the dangling, useless legs of the child, the enormous effort that was involved in this enterprise. I looked back up onto the sand and saw that the mother had set out two folding chairs and an umbrella for shade, an esky, towels. How many trips did it take, I wondered, to get all this and her daughter down to the sea?

I walked to the end of the beach and then turned back. By the time I reached the mother and daughter again, they were standing in the shallow water, feeling the waves lap around their feet. The mother held her daughter in a precious grasp, her face close to the child's ear, making cooing sounds of delight as one might soothe a baby who feared its first exposure to the sea. With one hand, the mother wiped away spittle that dribbled down from her child's slack lips.

I kept walking and I shivered with uneasiness. My mothering was coming to an end. This woman's mothering would have to go on forever. I wondered how I would behave if I were her. Would I have her courage? If that physically helpless child were mine, would I bring her down to touch and taste the sea? I thought I probably would.

Also available from Leone Sperling

COINS FOR THE FERRYMAN

ONE

She has come to visit me. Bundling, grey efficiency – severe-faced, square-jawed, high cheek-boned, rouged, slim-waisted, small-breasted, neatly packaged in round-necked, pastel-coloured, candy-striped dress – my mother.

It is Friday, 10am. Her eyes dart guarded glances at my untidy lounge room. The deep, soft, gold and maroon tapestry-patterned bean-bag chairs flop in comfortable disarray. I can almost discern, in their disordered curves, the imprint of the four little bodies that, last night, nested curled in their velvet warmth.

She looks around. Her hands itch. She picks up a doll with a vegemite face. She cannot hide her distaste. She longs to scream at me, wants to shout out her disgust, ask me how I can possibly live in such a filthy, unhygienic mess. She says nothing. She keeps herself in control. I want her to shout at me so that I can shout back at her. I want her to attack me so that I can defend myself. But in my family no one shouts. We keep our screams locked carefully below throat level. Our howls reverberate in our bellies. We never, never let them out.

'Would you like a cup of coffee?' I ask politely, showing that I know how to play the game, not allowing the aggressive 'What are you doing here? What do you want?' questions to rise any further than my navel.

She can't help it. While I'm putting on the kettle she has to gather the dirty breakfast dishes, scrape the greasy bits of bacon and half-eaten toast off the plates.

'I'll just wash up these few dishes, dear,' she says, 'while you're making the coffee.'

I want to tell her not to wash them up, but the words don't come out. I feel an angry scream mounting inside me but I squash it down and make a grab for a leftover piece of cold toast before it disappears into the rubbish bin. I half chew it and swallow it down quickly to keep the scream from surfacing.

'I thought I would come and give you a hand,' she says.

'I don't need any help,' I reply. Have I actually said the words? I'm not sure. Maybe they are just the words that I would like to be able to say. She goes on as if I haven't said them so I assume I've kept quiet.

'I thought,' she continues, 'that as you're going away on Sunday, you might need some help to get things cleaned up before you leave.'

'I don't need any help.' This time I'm damned sure I've said the words out loud, but she still goes on as if I haven't. I take the biggest apple I can see in the fruit bowl and tear off an enormous bite with my teeth. I keep chewing while she talks to me.

'You don't have it easy,' she says, you girls today. Not like my day. I always had a maid to help me. Look at you – divorced, alone with four children, a big house to run, a full-time teaching job. It's not easy, not easy at all.

I swallow my mouthful of apple and take a deep breath. I speak very loudly and very clearly. 'I don't need any help.' She looks hurt.

'Thanks very much for offering, Mum, but I can do it myself.' A year ago I couldn't have said it. A year ago I'd have let her bulldoze her way through our belongings and create order out of our chaos.

She sits down to drink her coffee. 'Well, dear,' she says, 'I'll just have a cup of coffee with you before I go.' I have defied her, but now some inner force compels me to open the biscuit cupboard. My hands take out the new packet of chocolate biscuits. My fingers tear off the cellophane wrapping and then from hand to mouth the biscuits go – shove, crunch, swallow.

She pretends not to notice what I'm doing in the hope of hiding her horror. She thinks that if she ignores what I'm doing then I'll stop doing it. She's wrong. I would like to be able to stop eating the chocolate biscuits but I don't know how to do that. She keeps on pretending that she's not watching me. But I know she's watching me and that makes it impossible for me to stop. She would like to grab hold of me and shake me and make me stop. She would like to scream, 'How can you be such a pig!' But she sticks to the rules, confining her scream to her eyes.

I think I'm going to vomit. I wish I would. But I know I won't. I never vomit. My stomach's made of elastic.

'You really need to get away, dear, don't you,' she says, sympathetically.

'Yes, I do,' I reply, struggling for control.

'You know, dear,' she goes on, trying not to count the exact number of biscuits I've eaten, 'when you get to London you must book yourself up on organized tours. Believe me, it's the only way to travel. That's what Daddy and I have found. Someone else does all the worrying for you. And you meet such nice people. People who speak your own language. I mean otherwise, dear, you might be very lonely, mightn't you, going overseas for six weeks all by yourself.'

I stare at her, through her. She goes on talking. I retreat. I don't know what she's talking about. Going overseas 'alone'. What does she mean? Doesn't she see that, on my life's journey, I am constantly accompanied by two grandmothers, three aunts, five cousins, one brother, one sister, one father, an ex-husband and four children? Above all, doesn't she realize that I always carry her iron-grey image around with me? Doesn't she understand that I'll be taking her overseas with me? Hopefully I'll lose her – somewhere along the way.

She leaves and I am alone with myself and my thoughts, my house and my mess to puddle and muddle and sift through and order. And I do it, in my own quiet, chaotic way. By the end of the day I have achieved a semblance of order that my children would regard as tolerable. If the dining room table is still piled high with the favourite possessions of four small people, then who cares? We never eat at the dining room table anyway. To the five of us, our mess connotes warmth, love, friendliness. Why should we care if it offends the eye of the outsider? We are snug and warm and secure in our sea of dolls and cars and guns and books and sticky, soft caresses.

My eyes fill with tears. I allow the trickling warmth to tumble down my cheeks. Can I bear to leave them, to be separate from them, for six whole weeks? How will they manage without me? I'm forty years old. Time, surely, to go off on my own for a while – to have a look at the world, to have a look at myself. Of course they can manage without me.

Time, too, I realize, to pick them up from school. It is the last dreary day before the long summer holidays begin. My three sons come bounding out of the gate. How little it takes to make their eyes shine – a hailstorm, a rainbow, an ice cream, the last day of school. I try to look at them objectively and can't. Surely anyone would find them beautiful. The oldest boy – large, placid, responsible, almond-eyed. The second – little, nuggety, tough, aggressive, black cherry eyes. The third – precious, gentle, sensitive, blonde-curled, soft-lipped. They all want to talk at once. It's impossible. I shout for silence, allot turns (youngest first) and each boy's news bubbles out. They are all high on holidays.

We pick up the littlest one. She is waiting anxiously. Tiny, exotic, dark-haired, delicate girl-child. I pick her up and hug her and feel her little arms about my neck. She tolerates my show of affection because she hasn't seen me all day. We bundle into the car and they talk excitedly of holidays and fun, of beaches and picnics, of films they want to see, of Christmas Day at Grandma's house, of presents they might get. Suddenly someone mentions the fact that I will not be there. An appalling silence descends upon us all.

★ ★ ★ ★ ★

'I understand,' she says, with absolute assurance, 'that you need to be on your own for a while. When I grow up, she goes on, 'I'll want to be alone for a while too.'

It is Sunday. 10am. The day I am due to leave on the grand world tour. She is sitting up on the bench next to me, while I wash up the breakfast dishes. She is six years old.

I don't know what to say to her.

'Will it upset you,' I ask, 'to stay with Grandma and with Daddy while I'm away?'

'Not at all,' she replies. She goes on, 'It's perfectly natural for you to want to be alone. You might,' she adds, 'even write some more stories while you're away.' I want to dry my hands, hug her, kiss her, tell her I love her, tell her it's not her I want to leave, tell her she must know how much I love her, explain to her that its just that I need to be alone for a while, need to sort myself out, see where I'm going. But she's not asking me for reassurance, she's not begging for love, so I can't give it to her.

I go on washing-up and I listen to the chatter.

Why is she so secure and why am I so insecure? My mother's words on the telephone half an hour ago still echo in my ears – 'Not coming to the airport … such a hot day …you don't mind, do you dear? …such big crowds … not coming to say goodbye.' I am shocked numb. I cannot believe she will not come.

I finish in the kitchen and go into my bedroom to pack my suitcase. I know exactly what I'm taking so it's not a difficult task to carry out. While I'm packing my mind goes back to yesterday.

It is Saturday. 1pm. It's my last full day with the children and I want them to be happy. 'Take us to Luna Park!' they all beg and plead. I hate Luna Park. I always refuse to take them there. I must be feeling terribly guilty about going away without them because I find myself agreeing to take them. They are unbelievably ecstatic.

As soon as we get there, they make me go on some dreadful machine that twirls me into space. I am quite sure I'm going to die. I can't even open up my eyes. They laugh at my terror. They get more pleasure from my fear than they do from the monstrous contraption we're riding on. I realize how afraid I am to leave the face of Mother Earth. Yet my children can leave it with defiant laughter, positive that no harm will come to them.

They make me go on the Ferris wheel. I'm not too bad while it's moving, but it keeps stopping to let more people on. Every time it stops I feel an overwhelming urge to jump off and smash myself on the ground below. I cling on to the two littlest children as if their tiny hands can hold my compulsion down.

They look at my terror. They shriek delightedly to each other, 'Look at Mummy! She's so scared she has to hold on to us. Look at her! Look at her!'

'Don't move!' I yell at them. 'Don't move! You'll fall!' They are doubled up with laughter. The more they laugh the more they move. The more they move the more terrified I become.

I see all five of us – a mound of indecipherable arms and legs, blood, flesh, brains emptying onto the pavement.

Thank God! It's not going to stop any more – it's going to keep moving. We just might survive after all. I find it's alright when the wheel is coming downwards towards the ground but when I am drawn upwards, away from the earth, my entire being shrieks a silent protest. The ride ends. They have to help me off. I am totally disordered. They sit me down. Their laughter turns to concern. They fuss over me. 'Are you alright, Mum?' 'Do you feel sick?' 'Can I get you a drink?' I am so shattered I cannot even reply. This is ridiculous. I don't want to frighten them. This is their day. We are all supposed to be having fun. With enormous effort I pull myself back to them. I laugh at myself. 'What a stupid mother I am, to be so afraid of heights.'

They are reassured. They like me to see myself in the role of 'stupid mother'. It makes them feel more grown up. I send them off with a few dollars to buy themselves ice creams while I get on quietly with the process of knitting myself together again. By the time they get back I'm all in one piece.

I've been 'good' so far today. Being 'good' means eating healthy foods, like meat and eggs and fruit and vegetables. Being 'good' means eating no bread and no cakes and no sweets and no chocolate biscuits. I've found, to my great surprise, that there's a health food shop at Luna Park. You can actually buy yoghurt instead of hot-dogs and fairy-floss. I'm pleased with myself for having been 'good' today.

My daughter suddenly hands me a sticky, dripping ice cream. 'I've had enough,' she says. Its melting sweetness is inside my mouth before I realize what's happened. One mouthful is all it needs for me to lose the battle for the day. For the rest of the afternoon I join the children on an endless orgy or waffles, ice cream, hot chips, soft drinks, lollies and fairy-floss until we all stagger to the car. They are full, warmly satisfied. A great day. I am bloated with despair. If I cannot cope with a Ferris wheel, how the hell am I going to cope with a jumbo jet?

I come back to my bedroom and my packing and to the two biggest boys bursting into my room, asking me how much money I'll give them to spend at the airport.

They are so calm. They behave as if today were any ordinary day. I feed on their tranquility and realize that they are quite able to let me go. They know I'll come back. They know that our circle of loving will always be there – warm, complete, secure.

How I wish I could be like them, but my mother's words are still banging away there inside my head – 'Not coming to the airport' – and I am forced to face the extraordinary truth that not one of my children is bound to me as I am bound to her.

They help me put my things in the car and we go off for our final treat. We are going to a Chinese restaurant for lunch and afterwards to the airport. My plane is due to leave at 4pm.

They love Chinese food and I don't mind taking them because it's always possible to be 'good' at a Chinese restaurant. I'm happy to stick to meat and vegetable dishes. Not like McDonald's. That's a nightmare. At McDonald's I am constantly faced with the temptation of Big Macs and French fries and ice cream sundaes with hot caramel sauce. At a Chinese restaurant I feel reasonably safe.

I'm very on edge. Anxiety. Terror. Anticipation. I remind myself, between the vegetable soup and the beef chop suey, that I've never been on my own for any sustained period of time. I have gone from belonging to belonging; from school to university to marriage; from parental home to marital home;

from being a child to being a wife to being a mother. There has never been a time when I have been responsible only to myself, belonged only to myself.

I feel that I ought to reprimand my third son, who is eight years old, for shoveling beef and oyster sauce into his mouth with a spoon and a hand instead of with a spoon and a fork. I stop myself. He is having such a marvelous time, gravy all over his hands and face. The frequent reprimands of my children's father momentarily disturb me, almost prompt me to tell my son to use his fork. 'Why can't you teach them some table manners! They can't even use a knife and fork properly.' He's right. They do embarrass him when he takes them out. But if I do reprimand my son it will be with his father's voice, not my own. He's not embarrassing me. I don't give a damn. I just enjoy watching his total immersion in messy pleasure. I win over the father's voice. I say nothing to my son. No! Damn it! I haven't won at all because suddenly I'm asking my daughter if she really wants all the rice she's ordered and she gives me some and before I know it I'm shoving rice into my mouth. Now I know for certain that when I buy them an ice-block after the Chinese meal, I'll have to buy one for myself as well. They'll be satisfied with water ice-blocks. I'm going to need an ice cream, probably with chocolate coating. I sink into despair. I am nothing but my mouth. I fuse with the food. I am the food. I cannot distinguish the boundaries of my self. I cease to exist. The avalanching, rumbling monster in my belly asserts himself again.

I try to picture him. He is a lion, roaring there in the dark hollow of my insides, demanding his right to gobble people up. I don't want him to gobble people up and, above all, I don't want anyone to know that he's inside me so I keep throwing him chunks of food to keep him quiet. I know I have to come to terms with him. If he and I are both going to inhabit this body for the rest of its life then we're going to have to understand each other. It seems to me that I'm always considerate about his needs but he doesn't make much effort to understand mine. At times I've thought of trying to exorcise him. But if I got him out of myself what would be left? How would I fill the gaping hole he left behind? Would there be anything left? Or am I synonymous with my lion; are he and I one entity and if I let him die would I die too? I don't know. So I keep on feeding him – just in case.

Am I mad? I don't really know but I don't think so. It all makes sense to me. I am born under the star of Leo and I carry my sign within me. A few times I've tried to tell people about it but when I do so I sense that they think what I'm saying is peculiar so I've learned to keep quiet about it, most of the time.

I don't just buy them ice-blocks. I become generous. I let them buy peppermint creams and thin, round, dark-chocolate discs from the expensive sweet shop that is just over the road from the Chinese restaurant. They can't believe their luck but my generosity is deceptive. I'm being cunning. I know that this shop sells mouth-watering Turkish Delight. My stomach is full but there is no connection between hunger and my need to eat. I have to have the sweet. I buy a whole pound. It's terribly rich. Any normal person would be satisfied with one or two pieces. I eat the lot. In five minutes it's all gone.

I want to vomit. I long to vomit. The rich, sticky sweetness nauseates me. I feel five months pregnant, my stomach distended and sore. I berate myself. 'You disgusting gluttonous pig,' I say to myself. I become the Turkish Delight, quivering, jelly-fat. I hate myself. I long for the day to be over. Tomorrow will be a new day, a new start, a new chance.

I always long for the magic of Mondays, a new beginning of a new week and if the first of the month happens to fall on a Monday then it seems to me that I have a double chance to start anew, to be 'good'. Maybe, just maybe, I will have the strength to get through a whole week, even a whole month, without stuffing myself with food. It never happens, of course. I'm so anxious about it being Monday that I'm usually shoveling food into myself by mid-morning.

I went to a hypnotist once. He stopped me from smoking and I thought he might be able to stop me from eating. It didn't work though. Sometimes, for no apparent reason, it goes away for a while and I actually stay on a diet for months and months. I get really slim and as soon as that happens I start eating again and put on all the weight I've lost. I once told myself that if it hadn't gone away by the time I was forty I'd kill myself. I'm forty now and it hasn't gone away. I can't very well kill myself though, can I? I've got four children relying on me.

And it happened again last night. It hasn't happened for years. I had a dream. People kept coming into my room, lots of people – my brother, my sister, Mum and Dad, men I've known. They held up a big white sheet next to my bed or maybe it was a flag – yes, that's right – an American flag or a Union Jack. I thought they might wrap me up in it. Perhaps it was my shroud. But they didn't. They just held it up so that I couldn't see behind it. I heard noises, though. I knew they were all screwing behind that flag and I was all alone; no one was making love to me and I felt so lonely that I started to cry and suddenly I couldn't breathe – I was choking, choking, choking and I woke up and I was suffocating, my face squashed in the pillow and I had to use every bit of strength I've got to force myself up on to my arms, to get my face out of the pillow that was smothering me, suffocating me, killing me. I was wide awake then, wet, shaking. I'll die that way. One day I'll dream my suffocating dream and it will really happen. I know that's the way I'll go back.

I've dreamed similar dreams ever since I can remember. At one time it frightened me so much that I wouldn't go to sleep. I was eighteen years old. I was sure I was going to die if I let myself go to sleep. She had to sit on my bed and keep me calm until I fell asleep. Like a mother should - for her baby.

She thinks I've forgotten but I haven't. I remember being born. No one believes me when I say that so it's another thing I've learned to keep quiet about. But I do remember. I remember before I was born too. I remember swimming soft in the sunlight of the womb, rocked gentle, lulled, swaying in her belly. I remember that I preferred to breathe through our chord, our harmony of food and air, complete and total flow. I never wanted to be born at all. She and I – so separate, so remote, so far from understanding each other; she and I were one once, tuned in to each other's needs. I moved when she moved, stopped when she stopped, started with fright at her fears, cried when she cried, laughed when she laughed. Fused together.

No wonder I resisted her efforts to expel me. I could not understand why I shouldn't stay in there forever. She'd been quite happy about our union for nine months, why did she now jerk and move the walls of my fortress, make them hard and rigid, drain away my soft fluid bed? Dry and harsh she became, forcing me movement by movement down her hostile canal, muscles contracting upon me, pushing, pushing, pushing me out into the stabbing air, the bright-lit sterility. And in her haste to rid herself of me she didn't even notice that she'd let the cord wind itself around my neck so that the moment of my birth was fired with harsh, rasping, choking strangulation. Life and death mingled at my cold awakening on that bleak August day.

When I was a child I often dreamed of being chased and strangled by a long pink snake lady. It was not so much the chase that frightened me, not even the strangulation. What frightened me was the end of the dream, the moment when I realized that the face of the snake lady was exactly the same as the face of my mother.

★ ★ ★ ★ ★

I am at the airport. Sunday 3pm. I feel so separate from myself that for a moment I can't understand what on earth I'm doing here. They want money for lollies, drinks, to play the games on the machines. I keep doling it out. I don't care what it costs, as long as they are happy, as long as they don't cry. Please, God, if you exist don't let them cry.

I go to the check-in counter. It's a sweltering day. My clothes are wet. I have to carry a heavy sheepskin coat. Suddenly I remember a dream I had a few nights ago. In my dream I was standing, just as I am now, waiting to check in before boarding the plane. In my dream it was terribly hot, just as it is today. In my dream they called out our flight number and then read out the London weather report – 'Sleet, snow, temperatures below zero, freezing, rain.' I looked down at my clothes and saw that I was wearing a thin cotton dress and realized, at the same moment, that I had left my sheepskin coat at home. 'I've forgotten my coat. I've got to go home and get my coat!' Although I shouted and screamed I was locked in the crowd and they carried me, coatless, onto the plane. I felt the terror of knowing that when I reached London I would inevitably freeze to death.

The shock of the dream shivers through me and despite the heatwave conditions I clutch my sheepskin coat fiercely to me.

I am at the head of the check-in queue. My hand wets the plastic folder that holds my ticket, passport, traveller's cheques.

'Ticket please,' she says. I give her my ticket. I am very neurotic about my passport. I hope she won't ask for it. The reason I'm so neurotic about my passport is that I went through such trauma to acquire it. The red tape involved in digging up certified copies of marriage and divorce papers was bad enough. So was the implied insult from the Officer in the Immigration Department who felt that no adult lady could possibly be only 143 centimetres in height. But, worst of all, was my trip to the Registrar General's Department where my request for a copy of my birth certificate was met with the extraordinary reply that my birth had never been registered.

'It has to be there,' I told them. They checked again. There is a record of my older brother's birth; there is a record of my younger sister's birth. I feel negated. Wiped out. Why did they forget to register my birth? I ask them why. They say to each other:

'I thought you did it, Mummy dear.'

'No, dear, it was always your job to register the births.'

'Where do you want to sit,' she asks, 'aisle or window seat?' I am about to say I don't care when my friend interrupts. He has come to the airport to say goodbye to me and to take my children back to their father's house. He has had a premonition that my plane will crash.

'She'll sit right at the back of the plane,' he interjects, 'in the last row.' He doesn't want me to go. He thinks he loves me.

He thinks I'll screw ten different men every day. He thinks I'll forget him. He might be right. So he's invented the idea that my plane will crash. The certain knowledge of my death has come to him in a dream. He's had other dreams like this before. They always come true. Normally such foreboding would terrify me, but this time it doesn't. I tell him again that the plane won't crash and that I refuse to die. I'm not sure that I believe what I'm saying but by now I feel swept along too far to turn back. I've got a real sense of inevitability right now. I just know that I am going to get on that plane and go.

My third little boy flings himself into my arms and has started to give me the 10,174 kisses that he has calculated he will require to see him through the next six weeks. He is the only one I am worried about. He seems to need me so much. I know the others are self-assured enough to cope. We peck at each other, little mouth kisses, lip to lip, endlessly building his fortress of love. I suddenly wonder how he'll manage to shit while I'm away. He has some anxiety about shitting. He never does it at school or at anyone else's place. He always waits for me. 'Start me off,' he says. That means I have to stand at the toilet door while he starts. After the first 'plop' he's safe and tells me I can go away. Can he go for six weeks without a shit? I don't suppose he can. It's better than it used to be. I used to have to sit on the floor outside the toilet and talk to him the whole time.

Sometimes he develops a compulsive sniff, or his eyes twitch, or he looks at the palms of his hands and then at the soles of his feet. The symptoms are always on the move. He never sticks to any of them for too long. And he can't drink any soft drink if anyone else has drunk out of the bottle and he can't eat his dinner if anyone else breathes on it. And, above all, he can't bear to look at straight arms. No one in the family is allowed to hold their arms out straight. I don't know why. But we all understand about his little peculiarities and he has managed to carve out for himself an area of tolerance that is given to no one else in the family. He gets migraines, too, but we all ignore them. He just lies upside down on the big bean-bag chair and falls asleep and he's all better in an hour or two. I've asked the other kids to look after him but will the adults who mind him understand? He lives on some other level of reality. He just visits us occasionally but whenever he comes to call he needs so much reassurance and love before he flits off again to his own, more interesting, realm of existence.

We're up to kiss number 764 when I suddenly hug him to me. Precious, curly-haired, ageless child. 'You'll be alright, won't you?' I ask fiercely.

'Seven-hundred-and-sixty-five, seven-hundred-and-sixty-six,' he goes on, unable to be distracted from his compulsive counting.

Everything to him is a matter of numbers. As soon as he meets someone he wants to know how old they are. He's not being rude. He just needs a new jumping off point for his endless calculations. The patter goes something like this: 'If you're twenty-four years old then you're three times as old as I am and you're fifty-two years younger than Grandpa and sixteen years younger than Mummy. You might think I'll never be half your age but when you're thirty-two, I'll be sixteen and then I'll be half as old as you are.' It doesn't stop there. It goes on and on. At first you feel some need to check his calculations. Then you realize you're not supposed to do that. There's no doubt that he's right. You just have to keep nodding your head and mumbling, 'Yes'. He can't read very well and when he writes he holds his pencil in such a peculiar way that his letters emerge on the page as a spidery code of hieroglyphics. He thinks he isn't clever. I suspect he's a genius. We are up to kiss number 801. I go on and on because that's what he needs and I resist the desire to crush my warmth and my love into his little body.

'That'll do,' he says. 'I don't need as many as I thought I did.' I am relieved. I have visions of myself not being able to board the plane because we have not reached the magical number that will set him free.

My friend stands beside me, bleak. As my flight number is called he hugs me to him and I feel his tears on my cheek. Then I start to cry and I am bewildered. The children do not cry and they do not understand why we do. I have been so worried that they would be the ones to break down and now the sight of this adult crying absolutely undoes me. I break away from him and give my children a final hug. The two smallest ones are silent. I sense their state of shock. 'Have a good time,' the two big ones say, almost in unison, embarrassed by my tears.

I look at her, the littlest. In her tense eyes I see the wish to rush after me. She grabs her biggest brother's hand. He helps her hold herself back. She would like to spring from the crowd of people and dive into the plane with me. My last sight is of her tiny face, lips firmly pressed, holding back. I can't risk turning around. I dare not look at them again.

AUTHOR'S BIOGRAPHY

Leone Sperling was born in Sydney in 1937, attended Sydney Girls' High School and graduated from Sydney University with a BA Honours degree in English literature. She taught English full-time with the NSW Department of TAFE for twenty years, a career that she found rewarding and fulfilling. She regards the fact that she did find time to write as a minor miracle because her marriage ended when her children were very young.

Three books, Coins for the Ferryman, Mother's Day and Oasis were published between 1981 and 1990. She was awarded a Literature Board grant in 1985. She has also had several short stories and articles published in national newspapers and Australian anthologies. These are now collected in The Book of Life.

After taking early retirement she wrote two novels, What About Love? and Jamie. She then undertook a four-year naturopathic Diploma in Nutrition. Leone now enjoys close, mutually rewarding relationships with her four children and six grandchildren and studies Latin with Continuing Education at Sydney University. Severe hearing impairment has resulted in the need for a Cochlear implant. For several years Leone has been on the Management Committee of Better Hearing Australia's Sydney branch and spends a considerable amount of time as a research volunteer with Cochlear and with the National Acoustic Laboratories.

Leone's writing is open and honest. Her style is spare and simple but constantly displays a willingness to confront and examine both the joyful and the darker aspects of human emotions and relationships.